"I Need You To Keep This A Secret."

Lie about not being the biological mother to keep the stability of a little family intact?

There was no question.

"Of course," she said. She offered a small smile to show she truly meant it, even as part of her wondered why such a thing would matter when other things were more important. But she pushed the thought aside—she wouldn't get involved in family dramas. It wasn't her place.

Some of the tension fell from his shoulders and one corner of his mouth lifted in a cheerless version of a grateful smile. Her heart bled for the anguish she'd just seen in the depths of his eyes. She forced herself to look out the window—she was here to help the boy, not the father. As much as everything inside her longed to soothe the lines of pain around his eyes, it was simply not her role.

Things were too complicated already.

* * *

Dear Reader,

I was thrilled to be invited to contribute to Dynasties: The Kincaids—the opportunity to work with a stellar bunch of authors was far too good to pass up. And when I was told it was Matthew Kincaid's story I'd be writing, I couldn't have been more excited.

Matthew is such a fabulous character—strong, noble and a loving father—that I was keen to spend time delving into his life and helping him meet his destiny in Susannah Parrish. And little Flynn? He just crawled right into my heart and didn't leave.

I also loved immersing myself in South Carolina and Charleston culture. I watched a heap of movies filmed there (a great excuse for a movie marathon!), listened to Southern bands when I was writing, researched the history and pored over blogs and webcams from Charleston. Now I have a teensy obsession and am planning to visit one day!

Special thanks to Kathie DeNosky, Jennifer Lewis, Heidi Betts, Tessa Radley and Day Leclaire for being a brilliant group of women to brainstorm and explore the lives of the Kincaids with, and thanks to Charles Griemsman for his most excellent guidance on the Kincaids series.

I hope you enjoy meeting Matthew, Susannah and Flynn as much as I did!

Cheers,

Rachel

RACHEL BAILEY

WHAT HAPPENS IN CHARLESTON...

Special thanks and acknowledgment to Rachel Bailey for her contribution to the Dynasties: The Kincaids miniseries.

ISBN-13: 978-0-373-73151-0

WHAT HAPPENS IN CHARLESTON...

Recycling programs
for this product may
not exist in your area.

www.Harlequin.com

Printed in U.S.A.

Books by Rachel Bailey

Harlequin Desire

Return of the Secret Heir #2118
What Happens in Charleston... #2138

Silhouette Desire

Claiming His Bought Bride #1992
The Blackmailed Bride's Secret Child #1998
At the Billionaire's Beck and Call? #2039
Million-Dollar Amnesia Scandal #2070

Other titles by this author available in ebook format

RACHEL BAILEY

developed a serious book addiction at a young age (via Peter Rabbit and Jemima Puddleduck) and has never recovered. Just how she likes it. She went on to earn degrees in psychology and social work, but is now living her dream—writing romance for a living.

She lives on a piece of paradise on Australia's Sunshine Coast with her hero and four dogs, where she loves to sit with a dog or two, overlooking the trees and reading books from her ever-growing to-be-read pile.

Rachel would love to hear from you and can be contacted through her website, www.rachelbailey.com.

For Cathy Bay,

who handed me my first category romance novel
("See what you think," she said); who was the first person
to say, "You should write a book;" who introduced me
to Romance Writers of Australia; who read and
critiqued my first writing efforts; and who has
given me the gift of sixteen years of friendship.
Cathy, this book (and the ones before it)
literally would never have eventuated without you.

Thanks to Barbara Jeffcott Geris, Robyn Grady and
Sharon Archer for reading drafts of this book and making
it better. I appreciate you all more than I can say.

Thanks to Charles Griemsman for the superb editing
and to Jenn Schober for her agenting skills.

* * *

Don't miss a single book in this series!

Dynasties: The Kincaids
New money. New passions. Old secrets.

Sex, Lies and the Southern Belle by Kathie DeNosky
What Happens in Charleston... by Rachel Bailey
Behind Boardroom Doors by Jennifer Lewis
On the Verge of I Do by Heidi Betts
One Dance with the Sheikh by Tessa Radley
A Very Private Merger by Day Leclaire

One

With his cell phone in a white-knuckled grip, Matthew Kincaid watched his son through the glass panel of the hospital room's door.

Three-year-old Flynn sat up against his pillows, his halo of dark hair haphazardly framing his little face. Two of his aunts, Matt's sisters Lily and Laurel, sat on either side of his bed, talking and playing with him. Since his wife's death a year ago, Matt's family had been extraordinary. They'd rallied around and given Matt and Flynn any extra support they'd needed.

It wouldn't be enough this time.

And all the wealth the Kincaids had amassed over three generations in shipping meant little in that room where his son was confined.

Despite the pale tone to Flynn's skin and the tired smudges under his eyes, onlookers might not guess how compromised his health currently was. Might not guess that his aunts had been through a decontamination process before being allowed in the private room, to avoid any germs gaining access to his weakened immune system.

As he watched his son try to learn the hand game Lily was teaching him—such a nice, normal activity for a little kid—Matt fought back the ball of emotion rising in this throat. He'd just come from a meeting with the doctors who'd laid out some chilling facts: Flynn's little body was still struggling to recover from the aplastic anemia. If his blood work didn't improve with the treatments they'd been using so far, they'd have to look at more drastic options.

Including a bone-marrow transplant.

A layer of ice settled over his skin, as it had done when the awful words had first been mentioned. Flynn was so young—too young to be facing such a procedure. And that was assuming they could even locate a compatible donor. The ideal option would be a sibling, but Flynn had none. Next best was a parent, but Matt's penicillin allergy had relegated him to being a last resort. The doctors didn't want to risk transferring the potentially life-threatening allergy to a three-year-old. Antibiotics were Flynn's only hope if he developed an infection.

Intellectually Matt could understand why the doctors didn't want to gamble on losing such a basic treatment—they'd explained in detail about documented cases of allergies transferred with marrow transplant. But it didn't make him feel any better. He wanted to be able to do something, *anything,* to help his little boy.

He curled his hand into a fist and pressed it to his solar plexus in a futile attempt to relieve the ache. When his son needed him the most, he'd failed him, and the knowledge was almost too much to bear.

He knew his brother and sisters would insist on being tested to see if they were a match, and Matt would welcome their offers, but the doctors had been pessimistic about the likelihood of a match being found there.

Which left only one option. One other person who had that primary link with Flynn. His biological mother.

He gripped the phone more tightly, took one last look at his little boy playing with his aunts and walked down the corridor to find some privacy.

Checking her watch, Susannah reached for the pages spurting from her printer. Twelve minutes till the meeting with the directors of the bank and the other key teams—since it was in an office down the hall, she'd easily make it. She'd stayed up late all week working on the new public-relations plan for the bank's rebranding, and was quietly confident they'd love it. Rebranding was a big move for the bank, and the PR angle was the biggest project Susannah and her team had handled, but they'd created strategies that were sure to get the reach they needed and generate a strong community buzz.

Her cell chirruped and she grabbed it as she slid the other arm into her jacket.

"Susannah Parrish," she said, scanning her desk to ensure she had everything for her presentation.

"Good morning, Susannah." The unfamiliar male voice was strained. "This is Matthew Kincaid."

The name immediately stilled her, brought a heaviness to her chest. Matthew Kincaid. Husband of Grace Kincaid, the woman to whom she'd handed her newborn baby. Memories of that day, of that special time in her life, crowded in, past the barrier she'd erected to keep them at bay—those few short hours she'd had with the newborn boy, his precious warmth and softness pressed against her. A sliver of time before she'd passed him to his new parents forever, giving them the gift of a baby, and saving her own mother from financial ruin.

Then her brain kicked into high gear.

"The baby," she whispered, her heart clutched tight. "Something's happened to the baby." There was no other reason he could be calling.

An uneven breath came down the line. "He's sick."

Sick? Her stomach swooped. He would only have turned three a couple of months ago. She dropped the folder on her desk and sank into her chair.

"What's wrong with him?" Though she hoped for something simple, logic dictated he wouldn't be calling over a head cold.

"He's had a virus," Matthew said, his voice sounding unnaturally rough, "and his body hasn't recovered properly."

That tiny little baby she'd nurtured in her womb was suffering. The thought was almost intolerable. "What can I do?"

"I was hoping you'd ask. There's an outside chance he might need a bone-marrow transplant. The best place to find a good match is a sibling or a parent, but I'm not an ideal donor." He paused and cleared his throat before continuing. "My brother and sisters will want to help, but—"

"How soon do you need me there?" she said without needing to think it through.

"You'll come," he said, as if confirming it aloud. And in those words she heard the massive relief he must be feeling.

"Of course I'll come. How soon?"

"The transplant isn't a definite yet—the doctors want to get the tests done and be ready to move if it does become necessary." There was a slight hesitation before he added, "But I'd appreciate it if you could come as soon as you can get away."

Pulse pounding through her body, she looked around her office, then at her watch again. She was owed time off, and her assistant was up-to-date and capable of covering for her. Taking leave without advance notice might cost her career a few points, but if that precious baby needed her, there was no contest. She could make this presentation, then hand everything over to her assistant and make a flight this afternoon.

She opened her bottom drawer and withdrew a vacation request form. "You're still in Charleston?" she asked.

"Yes. You're not?"

"Georgia now. I'll arrange leave immediately and get an afternoon flight." Her head was already buzzing with the arrangements and what she'd have to hand over to her assistant before she left the building.

"We could arrange for you to have the tests in Georgia." He spoke the words slowly and she heard his reluctance before he admitted, "But I'd prefer you to be here in case there's a crisis."

"I'd want that, too." Besides, she wouldn't be able to focus on anything here if she stayed while waiting on results. "Which hospital?"

"St. Andrew's, but send me your flight details and I'll pick you up from the airport."

Form in hand, she was on her feet, heading down the hall to her boss's office to get the request lodged before the presentation. "I'll ensure I'm there today."

"I'll see you then. And, Susannah," he said, voice deeper once again with emotion, "thank you."

"No need," she said as she knocked on her manager's office door, and ended the call.

Several hours later, she was wheeling her carry-on suitcase through the arrivals gate when she caught sight of Matthew Kincaid. At just over six feet, with closely cropped dark hair and a swimmer's body encased in a deep navy business suit, he was hard to miss. She remembered him clearly from a meeting she'd had with him and Grace before they'd signed the contract for surrogacy, and now, as then, he stole her breath.

However, she dismissed the reaction—it was irrelevant to her reason for being here.

His son.

Matthew saw her as she drew closer and gave her a tight nod of acknowledgment then reached for her suitcase. "I appreciate you coming so quickly."

"I'm glad to do it," she said truthfully.

The walk to the car was made in silence—she had too many questions to know where to start and Matthew appeared to be lost in his own world. During the pregnancy, she'd had much more contact with his wife—Grace's excitement about the baby had made her easy to talk to. Perhaps it would be best to save her questions for Grace.

She looked up at the blue Charleston sky. It had been almost three years since she'd been back. Georgia was where she chose to live, but Charleston was where she'd been born, where she'd grown up—it would always be home.

Once they were in his car and fastening seat belts, she asked, "Grace's with him now?"

A shudder seemed to race through his body, and then the only movement was the rise and fall of his chest as he looked through the windshield at the other parked cars, sunglasses hiding his eyes. He didn't turn to her as he spoke. "My mother is with him. Two of my sisters were there this morning but my mother swapped with them at lunchtime." A muscle in his jaw worked— he was so tense that she worried he would shatter into shards. Then he added, "Grace passed away a year ago."

Of its own volition, her hand lifted to cover her mouth, to smother the gasp that would otherwise have escaped. "How?" she asked from between her fingers then regretted it. The how was irrelevant when a man had lost his wife, and a little boy had lost his mother.

"Small plane crash." Still, he didn't look at her or make a move to start the car, simply sitting motionless in the shadowed light of the car's interior.

"Oh, Matthew, I'm sorry." She'd always thought of them as the perfect couple, a husband and wife with the world at their feet—gorgeous, rich, successful and in love. It seemed to go against the laws of nature for them to be so cruelly separated by death.

"Don't be sorry. It's not your fault." His words were loaded— he blamed someone for his wife's death, that much was clear. It was on the tip of her tongue to ask, but she had no right to pry any further into a topic that must cause intolerable pain. Having carried a child for this man did not alter the fact that she was a stranger. A stranger who needed to remember her boundaries and not be lulled into a false sense of intimacy because they had one thing in common. Matthew Kincaid deserved privacy in his grief for his wife.

Taking a mental step back, she sat up straighter in the plush passenger seat and brought the conversation around to the most pressing issue. "Tell me what's happening with Flynn."

With restless fingers, he tapped a rhythm on the steering wheel. "He had a parvovirus."

"I thought—" Feeling a little foolish, she stopped.

He tilted his head and looked at her. "That it was a virus dogs caught?" He gave a small, humorless smile. "I thought the same. There are lots of them, apparently, and Flynn caught a different strain. In children it can cause slapped-cheek syndrome. And that's just what it looked like—as though someone had slapped the poor kid's cheeks. Apart from that it seemed like he had pretty mild flu symptoms. Nothing out of the ordinary."

"But…?" she asked when he paused.

He rubbed a thumb across the grooves indented in his forehead. "But he didn't recover fully. He was lethargic and tired and just not himself. When I took him to the doctor they did some tests and found his white blood cells were low. Not critical, but by the next test they were even lower. They just kept dropping. The doctors said they expected the problem to be transient. That his bone marrow would start producing again." He grimaced. "But it hasn't."

"Have they tried other treatments?" she asked, but knew they must have if they were contemplating something this drastic.

Matthew nodded once. "They haven't had much effect so far. The doctors suggested screening the family for a compatible donor. In these cases the best possibility for a match is a sibling with the same parents. Next best chance are parents. After that the chances of compatibility get less."

"Which is where I come in."

"Which is where you come in," he echoed, lifting his sunglasses to sit on his head and turning to her. "He doesn't have a sibling and my penicillin allergy means they're reluctant to even consider me as a match at this stage." He spoke the last words almost through gritted teeth.

"You need his biological mother," she said, then bit down on her lip, feeling strange. She hadn't used that term to describe herself since the day she'd given birth to him and needed to fill out forms. She'd always felt good about giving him to such a loving couple, and considered him Grace and Matthew's child.

Now, just Matthew's.

His jaw clenched and released. "In retrospect, it was lucky Grace's eggs wouldn't take and we used yours. If they had, our options would be greatly reduced."

She swallowed. Grace had been hit hard by her inability to carry a child, but finding she couldn't use her own eggs, that she wouldn't be the biological mother of her own child, had devastated her. Grace had come to her, offering more money to contribute her eggs, but it hadn't been the extra money that had swayed her. Having lost a baby when she was younger, Susannah knew the value of the gift of life.

Matthew cleared his throat. "There's one more thing."

His tone sent a wave of trepidation through her veins. "Something else is wrong?"

"Not with Flynn. My family—and Grace's parents—believe that, although we used a surrogate, Grace was..." The shadowed skin of his jaw and throat pulled tight as he clenched the muscles there. "Grace wanted people to believe he was her baby in every way."

Having seen Grace's all-encompassing need to be a mother, she wasn't surprised that this was how they'd handled it. "It's okay, I understand."

His dark brows swooped low over green eyes sparkling with an intense honesty. "We meant no disrespect to you."

"None taken." She found a smile to reassure him. On this

point, at least, she could offer solace. "I'm not a part of his life, and Grace wanted him so very much."

"She did," he said, but the words were anything but simple. They carried a crushing weight with them. Her chest ached to witness such pain.

She looked more closely at this man who was raising the child she gave birth to. His broad shoulders were as rigid and set as if they'd been carved from marble. How heavy a load had they been carrying? Every instinct inside her demanded she reach out, to soothe. Instead she folded her hands in her lap to ensure they didn't move.

"Honestly, Matthew, I don't mind. I handed over that little baby to you and Grace with love. You don't need to explain anything to me about the decisions you've made."

"I appreciate that. Because I have something else to ask." He drew in a long breath and held it for a moment. "If you cross paths with my family, you'll find they can be…curious. Protective. And if they ask questions, you'll have the lead-in to tell them about your connection to Flynn." He turned to her, expression inscrutable. "I need you to keep Grace's secret."

Lie about not being the biological mother to keep the stability of a little family intact? With Flynn's health in question, instability and confusion were the last things they needed.

"Of course," she said. She offered a small smile to show she truly meant it.

Some of the tension fell from his shoulders and one corner of his mouth lifted in a cheerless version of a grateful smile, then he dropped the glasses back over his eyes and turned the key in the ignition. As the engine roared to life, her heart bled for the anguish she'd just seen in the depths of his eyes. She forced herself to look out the window—she was here to help the boy, not the father. As much as everything inside her longed to soothe the lines of pain around his eyes, it was simply not her role. Things were too complicated already.

* * *

Darkness was falling outside when Susannah made her way down the brightly lit hospital corridor to Flynn's room. Matthew had told her to find him there when her tests were over, and now she stood for a few moments observing them through the glass panel. Matthew's face was different with his son—the planes and angles looked softer, his smile easier. Yet the more tender version of Matthew Kincaid was just as compelling, perhaps more so. Her heart picked up speed and she couldn't tear her gaze away.

The little boy was facing away from her, so all she could see was a mop of dark brown hair and sweet little arms that reached out for his father's thumbs in whatever game they were playing. Then Matthew looked up and saw her and the tension seemed to pour into his body again until even his smile for Flynn seemed rigid. He said something to his son before pointing to the next room. She looked over and there was an interconnected door to Flynn's room so she headed over. Inside the anteroom was a washbasin, shelves of neatly folded gowns and boxes of masks and other paraphernalia.

The door opened and Matthew appeared. "He's being kept in semi-isolation," he said, answering her unasked question. "Before anyone goes in, they need to wash their hands up to the elbows and put on a gown." Something of her concern must have shown on her face because he shrugged one shoulder and said, "I'm just grateful he's not at the stage of needing us to wear a mask like the little girl in the room on the other side."

She looked through the glass panel to Flynn in his bed, curled up talking to a teddy bear. "He looks too small—too vulnerable—to be here."

Matthew didn't reply, but from the corner of her eye she saw him grimace. It must be beyond frustrating for him to watch his son in need and not be able to do anything about it. She fingered the strip of tape and bump of cotton on the inside of her elbow where they'd taken the blood, and prayed she'd be able to help if the transplant was needed.

"They're checking to see if I'm a tissue match now," she said, still watching the small boy interact with his teddy. "The woman who took the sample said they'd hurry it through and let us know preliminary results as soon as possible."

She felt Matthew nod, then they stood side by side for endless minutes, watching a three-year-old boy who'd already known too much pain in his short life, have a solemn conversation with a brown bear. The echoes of her hammering heart reverberated through her body, and the weight of all that rode on her tissue-matching test hung in the air, engulfing them in the small room.

"Would you like to meet him?" Matthew asked, his voice rough.

In one long whoosh, her lungs emptied. Even though she'd come here to help Flynn, she hadn't allowed herself a second's contemplation of being given the chance to meet him. Yet now the possibility was before her, as alluring as it was, she could see it was a bad idea. "It would just confuse things."

"We can keep it simple. We'll tell him you're a friend of mine and you wanted to say hello."

A little flame of excitement lit in her chest. Dare she meet this little boy? She'd willingly handed him to his new parents, never expecting to see him again—the situation of her own childhood had taught her it was better for children to have issues of custody and belonging mapped out and clear-cut.

But, he was within her sight—something she'd never dreamed would happen. And if they could keep it uncomplicated and clear…

The flame of excitement in her chest flickered and grew.

Dare she?

She looked to Matthew for a sign, and he seemed happy enough to allow the meeting. To give her something she could always treasure—a sliver of time with the boy she'd carried for nine months.

A smile crept across her face and she bit down on her bottom lip in an attempt to contain it.

"Thank you. I'd love to meet him."

Two

Susannah tentatively followed Matthew into his son's hospital room with its sky-blue walls and bunches of shiny balloons. Flynn looked so small sitting on the bed in his teddy-bear pajamas. He had a cannula in the back of his little hand that was bandaged but wasn't connected to anything at the moment. The idea of an IV attached to him made her chest clench.

Flynn's little pale face looked up and he threw out his arms. "Daddeeee."

Matthew gently swung him up and planted a kiss on his cheek. "I told you I wouldn't be long," he said with such love it made her heart clench tight.

Flynn's gaze slid over to her and Susannah held her breath. He was a miniature version of Matthew down to the same shaped eyes, the same full bottom lip, but he had a dimple in his chin. Like the one that punctuated her own father's chin. Like the one she had. The floor tilted beneath her, but she didn't take her eyes from Flynn as the reality hit her hard.

This little boy was half *her*.

She'd been so glad to be able to give the gift of parenthood to two people who were desperate for a baby, and so adamant that she keep everything compartmentalized in her mind, that she'd never dwelled on the fact that Flynn was made from her flesh and blood. A part of the family line that came from her mother and her lost father.

Even when she'd been considering meeting him moments earlier, it had been as if talking about someone else's child, one she'd heard stories about. Not her mother's grandchild. Not her father's grandson.

Solemn blue eyes regarded her, then he asked his father in a loud whisper, "Who's that?"

And just like that, her heart was captured, and she had to blink back tears.

"This is a friend of mine." Matthew turned so Flynn was facing her. "Her name is Susannah."

"Hello, Flynn," she said past the lump in her throat.

"Hello, Sudann—" he frowned as he tried to wrap his tongue around the name "—Sood..."

"Maybe we could try something easier?" Matthew said, raising a dark eyebrow. It was a simple move, yet it transformed his face into something edgier, more alluring. Her mouth went dry. She looked back to Flynn, determined not to react to the innate appeal of his father, and found another Kincaid male who was hard to resist.

Interlacing her fingers over her belly so she wouldn't reach out to touch his little face, she smiled softly. "When I was little, my dad called me Suzi."

"Sudi," Flynn said.

She couldn't help but beam, hearing the baby she'd help create say her name. Or something approximating it. "Perfect."

Matthew put the little boy back down on his bed then leaned close to her. "Would you mind sitting with him for a few minutes?" he asked quietly, his breath warm on her ear. "I have to call the office and it might be tense. Flynn is pretty good at picking up things like that and it's the last thing he needs right now."

The crisp, clean scent of his aftershave curled around her, creating a powerful distraction from his words, and, although he wasn't touching her, the skin near her ear tingled as though he had.

She swallowed. "We'll be fine."

"Thanks." He dropped a kiss on the top of his son's head and spoke in a normal voice again. "I just have to call Uncle RJ. And while I'm gone, Suzi is going to stay with you."

"Okay," Flynn said, looking at her with those large eyes that she suspected saw too much.

Matthew paused at the door and smiled, but there was tension around his mouth, around his eyes. "I'll be quick."

After he left, Susannah stared down at the boy who was part her and part Matthew, and wanted so much to bundle him up and hug him tight. Instead she said, "So, Flynn, what can we do for fun in here? Got any good books?"

"A teddy-bear book," he said as if they were discussing a deadly serious topic.

"Why, I love teddy-bear books! Would you mind if I read it out loud?"

The little boy blinked then climbed down and retrieved a large hardcover with beautifully painted teddies on the front and deposited it in her lap. "It's an Aunty Lily book," he said and Susannah saw "Illustrated by Lily Kincaid" on the cover. Then he crawled back up on the bed and sat against the headboard, waiting.

Susannah read the story—sneaking glances at him whenever she could—and at the end, Flynn graced her with a blinding smile—the first he'd directed at her. "Thank you, Sudi."

Her heart stilled as if it couldn't take the beauty of that innocent smile, but it didn't take her long to regroup. She gathered his warm little body closer and pressed her lips to his forehead. Flynn relaxed into her embrace so she allowed herself to hold the kiss longer. Tears welled in her eyes, but she had her lids shut tight and wouldn't let them escape. She didn't need forever, but she was going to savor every moment she had with him now.

Eventually, not wanting to make Flynn uncomfortable, she took a breath and released him. He hadn't squirmed, and now he simply looked up at her with a curious expression. She smiled and blinked away the moisture in her eyes.

"What would you like to do?" she asked, looking at the toys and puzzles piled on a little table. "Would you like me to read you another book? Or we could do a puzzle?"

Flynn sucked his bottom lip into his mouth, clearly assessing her before sharing his thoughts. Then he curled a finger, inviting her to lean down. When her ear was level with his mouth, he whispered, "Can you sing me a song?"

Her singing talents owed more to enthusiasm than any semblance of skill, but she didn't think a three-year-old would mind. "Sure," she said brightly. "Twinkle, Twinkle?"

Slowly, not losing eye contact, he shook his head. The look on his face told her he had something specific in mind, so she waited.

His finger called her down for another secret. "Do you know Elvis?"

A smile tugged insistently at the corners of her mouth but he was so serious she restrained it. "Not personally, but I know his songs. Would you like me to sing one of them?"

Eyes so filled with hope that it made her heart ache, he nodded.

"Any song in particular?"

"I like them all," he said and she wondered exactly how many Elvis songs a three-year-old could possibly know.

"Okay, then." Her mind flicked through Elvis's songbook

and decided to try "Love Me Tender"—well-known and simple. As she sang the first couple of lines, a huge grin spread across Flynn's face and he snuggled into her side.

At the end of the first verse, she paused. "More of this song, or another one?"

"This one," he said with conviction. "Sudi, you sing it right."

She tilted her head to the side—her singing voice was hardly the best he would have heard, so what else could "right" mean? "Who doesn't sing it right?"

Warily he glanced over to the door then, apparently satisfied he wouldn't be overheard, he said in a stage whisper, "Aunty Lily sings it fast. And she dances."

Susannah had to hold back a laugh. Aunty Lily sounded fun. "So we don't want a dance version?"

He frowned as if that were an obvious point.

"Right, no dance versions of Elvis. Is Aunty Lily the only one who doesn't sing it the way you want?"

"Daddy sings them sad."

Without meaning to, she looked at the door where she'd last seen Matthew and her heart twisted. Why would Elvis make him sad? Perhaps an Elvis song had been Matthew and Grace's personal song? Or did he always sing sadly?

"Can you sing more?" Flynn asked, interrupting her thoughts.

"Sure I can, sweetie." She picked up the second verse, careful not to make it too fast or too sad, and her heart swelled when Flynn cuddled back into her side again.

As Matt strode down the corridor toward the anteroom, he caught a glimpse of a scene that had him slowing his steps then stilling. Susannah sat on his son's bed, Flynn curled against her slender body as she sang to him. Her head was dipped, her long blond hair partially curtaining them both. He couldn't hear the words, but knowing Flynn, he'd requested the Elvis songs Grace used to sing him. A chill crept across his skin.

The singing itself didn't surprise him—Flynn was remarkably proficient at convincing people to sing to him—it was his son's posture. Relaxed. Content. Trusting.

Since Grace's death, there hadn't been a single new person that Flynn had become affectionate with before he came to know them.

What had she said to inspire trust so quickly?

Part of him was glad that Flynn had found this ability to trust again, but another part wanted to drag Susannah away before his son became attached. The last thing that little boy needed was to lose someone else he'd come to love. The tight band that had been squeezing his chest for weeks now constricted that much more. Perhaps it had been a mistake to let her in his son's room.

He ran a hand through his hair and blew out a breath. He'd work out what to do about Susannah and Flynn's relationship later. For now, he had plans to make. He went in through the side room, washing his hands to the elbows, took a fresh gown, and when he slipped into the room, he found he'd been right about Elvis—Susannah was singing "Blue Suede Shoes." Her crystalline-blue eyes shone, her voice was sweet and she made him think of crisp, white sheets bathed in sunlight. Of stretching her out on those sheets and tasting the expanse of creamy skin he'd uncover.

Restraining a groan, he clenched his fists and forced the inappropriate thoughts from his mind. Not *this* woman, who his wife had envied but had understandably resented in equal measure. Nothing would betray his wife's memory more than him desiring Susannah Parrish.

Besides, between Flynn's hospitalization and Matt's recently discovering that his dead father had a second family on the side—and had left stock in the family business divided amongst the legitimate and illegitimate siblings—Matt didn't have the headspace to deal with one more thing. He needed to stay focused.

Susannah looked up and saw him but her singing didn't falter. Flynn's eyes were closed and when Matt crept closer, he saw his son had the deep, even breaths of sleep. He motioned to Susannah with a hand under the side of his head that Flynn was asleep then pointed to the other side of the room.

While she continued to sing, albeit in a softer voice, Matt picked his son up, moved him to the center of the bed and pulled the covers over him. This little boy was the most precious thing in his life and it killed him inside that he couldn't simply kiss him and make him better the way he'd been able to do until now. The doctors weren't even keen to let him be a donor because of his damn allergy. He brushed the hair off Flynn's pale face, pulled himself together, then crossed to the other side of the room with Susannah.

"I just spoke with the doctor," he said, digging his hands into his pockets. "They expect the results to be here in the morning."

Her long lashes swept down and her shoulders stiffened, as if bracing herself for tomorrow's outcome. "I'll meet you here first thing. My suitcase is in your car—just drop me at whichever hotel is closest."

Matt took a deep breath. The hospitality his mother had taught all her children wouldn't allow him to take her to a hotel. Not when she'd traveled interstate to help his son. But how comfortable would she be staying in a house alone with a man she barely knew? And should he ask a woman home who, with no effort, had brought his body back to life?

The most logical answer was to take her to his mother's house. His mother enjoyed hosting guests and, Pamela, the housekeeper who'd always been so much more, would appreciate having someone else to fuss over.

But he couldn't do that.

His mother—his entire family—believed Grace was Flynn's biological mother. He couldn't tell them why Susannah was here, or that she was being tissue matched to the youngest Kincaid.

When they ran into various members of his family, which they inevitably would if the tissue match was positive and she stayed longer, he'd use a cover story. But running into someone when he was by her side and staying in his mother's house were two totally different situations. Could he trust Susannah not to slip up under those circumstances? He didn't know much about her and had no idea how well she lied.

Best not to put her in a testing situation. Which only left one option.

He cleared his throat. "You can stay with me."

"No, I'll be fine at a hotel," she said, waving his suggestion away with a hand. "Honestly."

"Nonsense. My mother would be horrified if I made you stay at an impersonal hotel when I have plenty of room."

A line appeared between her eyebrows. "I—"

He rolled his shoulders back, not prepared to negotiate on this point. "I won't take no as an answer. My sister Kara will be here in about ten minutes to stay with Flynn for the evening, so we'll go then."

Her head tilted to the side. "You have a schedule?"

"Of course. Flynn is the only grandchild in our family. Everyone is concerned." It was breaking his heart that he couldn't be at the hospital full-time, but the family business was in serious trouble, both from lost business and potential hostile maneuverings, and Flynn loved his aunts, uncles and grandmother, so Matt had compromised by sharing the time with his family. From the corner of his eye, he saw his sister already in the anteroom next door, a little early as usual. "Kara made a timetable—her organizational skills are superb. Here she is."

The moment Kara stepped into the room, he wrapped her in a bear hug. "Thanks."

She held up an overstuffed bag. "We'll have fun—I made play dough and bought him his own set of highlighters for coloring. Hopefully that means he'll stop pinching mine." She grinned.

He grinned back. He could always count on Kara. "You know you're my favorite sister."

She laughed and rolled her eyes at Susannah. "He says that to all of us."

Susannah smiled as she looked back and forth from Kara to him. "How many sisters are there?"

"Three," Kara said. "We outnumber the brothers—there are only two of them."

As soon as she said it, she stiffened and Matt felt the same tension fill his muscles. There *had* been two brothers. Until his father's death, when they found they had a half brother they'd known nothing about. A secret big enough to become a betrayal of the entire family.

Shaking his head to dispel the thoughts, he touched a hand to Susannah's elbow. "Kara, this is Susannah, an old friend of Grace's."

Susannah didn't flinch at the way he'd introduced her, which he appreciated. He'd have liked to discuss their story before she met any of his family, but fortunately she seemed able to roll with the punches.

Kara reached out to shake her hand. "Nice to meet you, Susannah. Are you here to see Flynn?"

"Yes," Susannah said, no trace of artifice or nerves. "I was in town and gave Matthew a call. He mentioned Flynn was unwell and I wanted to visit."

A warmth glowed in his chest that stemmed from appreciation and respect for her quick thinking.

"Grace would have liked that," Kara said.

"Actually," Susannah said, "Matthew mentioned that you'd made a schedule to ensure someone is with Flynn. I'll be here at least a couple of days, maybe longer, depending on how a few things pan out, and I wouldn't mind helping out if you need someone else."

The tight band around his chest constricted. The more time

Susannah spent with Flynn, the more his son would become attached—laying the groundwork for a disaster when she left.

"That would be fabulous," Kara said. "Nights and weekends are no problem, but sometime during business hours would work well if that suits you? Our mother and Lily are the only ones who can easily arrange their days, so the schedule gets a bit tight then."

Matt rubbed the tight muscles at the back of his neck. How could he refuse an offer that would give his family a break? They were all going above and beyond for Flynn and he was more grateful than he could ever say. He dropped his hand from his neck and stuffed it in a pocket. It would only be a few days and he'd talk to Flynn if things got out of hand. He took a small step back to let them make the arrangements.

"I can start tomorrow," Susannah said.

"Great." Kara pulled an electronic organizer from her bag and began tapping buttons. "Just give me a number I can contact you on."

Before Susannah could revisit the idea of staying at a hotel, he cut in. "I've invited her to stay at my place while she's here. You can reach her there."

There was a flicker of a question in Kara's eyes before she seemed to dismiss it. "Perfect, I'll be in touch. But now, there's a gorgeous little boy just waking up, so I'd better go over and say hello."

Twenty minutes later, after he'd said goodbye to his son, he and Susannah were in his car, on the road to his house.

He squared his shoulders, ready to open a difficult conversation. "I apologize for lying about your relationship back there."

"Matthew," she said gently, "this is *your* family, your life—yours and Flynn's. I'm here to help. You do whatever you need to do and I'll fit in."

He wasn't used to such unqualified support. Grace had often been quite contrary, and his family was loving but opinionated—everyone having their two cents' worth at family lunches. Susannah's willingness to let him choose the path here, without question, was as welcome as it was novel.

He glanced over—her delicate features were relaxed and open, confirming there was no undercurrent to her words, and he had a feeling that what you saw was what you got with Susannah Parrish. "I appreciate that."

"Though, it would help if we talked about it so we're on the same page."

"Agreed," he said as he smoothly took a corner. "I should have mentioned it before we ran into Kara, but we covered well."

"So, I'm an old friend of Grace's?"

"It's not strictly a lie." He could feel her gaze on him and, after stopping at traffic lights, he turned to her. Her eyes were the blue of a summer's sky, and just as endless. It was the first thing he'd noticed when she'd approached him in the airport. A man could lose himself in eyes like those. He frowned and dragged his gaze back to the red light. "You and Grace spent time together several years ago."

"They don't know anything about Flynn's surrogate?"

"They don't know your name, so my family won't suspect it's you. Grace wanted details kept to a minimum since it reminded her too much of what she perceived as her failure." Nothing he'd said to her had been able to sway her from that assessment of herself. She'd been an excellent mother to Flynn. Genetics paled into insignificance compared to that.

The light turned green and he smoothly pressed down on the accelerator. "And if we tell them you're the surrogate, without telling them you're also the biological mother, they'll wonder why you're here since a normal surrogate wouldn't be needed in this situation."

"So we keep it simple?"

He'd put a lot of thought into this since the moment he'd known he'd have to call her. It was the only plan that seemed reasonable. "It's our best option."

"What if the tissue matching is positive and Flynn needs the transplant? Won't that make it harder to hide?"

"We'll cross that bridge if we have to." And he was praying like crazy that they never had to. He swallowed hard and his hands gripped the wheel tightly. "But my family—no one—can ever know that Grace isn't Flynn's biological mother."

He'd made a vow to Grace that he would not break. In fact, he was doubly bound to keep that vow—since he'd as good as killed her by making her take the fatal plane flight, the only means he had left to honor his college sweetheart was to protect her secret. He owed her this, and so much more.

The drive through Charleston brought back a multitude of memories from when she'd lived here. Susannah glimpsed the grand old houses the city was known for, standing tall and elegant as they passed; the bustle of downtown; the majestic trees draping the sidewalks. Sweet nostalgia filled her soul—she'd rarely been back to her hometown since the move to Georgia three years ago and she'd missed it.

A few blocks from where the Peninsula met the sea, Matthew pulled into the driveway of what looked like an overgrown stone cottage with large windows on both stories and a creeping vine covering large portions of the downstairs walls.

After opening the door, he stepped back to allow her to enter and Susannah took an uneven breath. She was merely staying with Flynn's father so she could be on hand if she was needed. It was a practical plan that made complete sense.

So why did it feel dangerous?

Some fanciful part of her was reacting as if an attractive man was inviting her back to his place because he was interested in her. Which was ridiculous. Just *how* ridiculous, she realized once she'd stepped over the threshold. The first thing that greeted her was a large framed photo of Grace, smiling beatifically, with baby Flynn in her arms. And, as he guided her through the house, she found more photos covering the walls.

Photos of Grace with Flynn, with Matthew, or the three of them together. Large and small; snapshots and portraits; laughing faces and soft, dreamy expressions.

This was not the house of a man who would ever invite another woman home. This was the house of a man still deeply in love with his wife.

Matthew stopped in front of a door, opened it and switched on the light. In the middle of the large room stood a four-poster bed, with lace fringing and a quilted cover in soft pinks and mauves.

"This is the guest bedroom. The bathroom is through there," he said, pointing to a door leading directly from the bedroom. "I'll give you a few minutes to freshen up, then, when you're ready I'll find us something to eat in the kitchen."

She'd eaten lunch on the plane, but nothing since. At his words, her stomach rumbled. "I can fix something if you want."

His gaze flicked to her stomach then back to her face with a faintly amused quirk at the edge of his full bottom lip. "No need. Pamela, my mother's housekeeper, keeps a stock of home-cooked meals in my freezer."

"That's sweet of her." For reasons she wasn't prepared to examine too closely, she was glad that Pamela and the Kincaid family were looking out for Matthew and Flynn.

"She's done it since Grace passed. I think she's worried I'm too busy to cook."

"And you're not?" she asked, thinking of all he had on his plate.

A rueful smile twitched on his lips. "Usually I am. I say a prayer of thanks often for Pamela's thoughtfulness."

"If I end up staying a few days," she said, seeing the answer to something that had been playing on her mind, "I'd like to pull my weight. I'll do the cooking."

"Susannah, I think what you've offered to do for Flynn more than 'pulls your weight.'" He smiled even as he frowned, and the unusual combination tugged at her. "Don't worry about it. Kitchen is down the stairs to the left—I'll see you in ten."

She watched his tall frame stride down the hall, entire body taut with the responsibility that sat astride his broad shoulders. How exhausting must it be for Matthew to be the sole caregiver for Flynn when he still grieved for his wife? If only she could—

Stopping the thought before it went any further, she slipped back into her temporary bedroom and changed her clothes then splashed water on her face. This little family unit wasn't part of her life. She'd be leaving soon. She twisted her long hair up into a knot and secured it with a clip.

Feeling refreshed, she followed the stairs down to the kitchen to find Matthew minus his tie and with sleeves rolled to a couple of inches above his wrists, stirring a pot on the stove. Those masculine wrists and the light covering of dark brown hair on the glimpse of his forearms were mesmerizing, and for timeless moments she couldn't drag her gaze away.

"I hope you like chili beans," he said as he looked up. "I'm reheating one of Pamela's specialties."

"Love them," she said, giving herself a shake to recover her equilibrium. She leaned closer to the pot. "Smells good. Can I do anything?"

He passed her an oven mitt. "The corn bread's ready to come out of the oven."

"I was serious, by the way," she said as she slid the tray of bread onto the marble kitchen island. "If I need to stay, I won't feel comfortable with you housing and feeding me unless I'm doing something. Besides, I've taken a week's leave and even with visiting Flynn sometimes at the hospital, I might go crazy with boredom."

"Well, I'd hate to cause someone to lose their sanity." An eyebrow arched in faint amusement. "I'm only willing to consider the possibility that the tissue matching will be positive, so, as far as I'm concerned, you're staying awhile. You can do some of the cooking. I'll leave the keys to Grace's Cadillac and a credit card. You'll need ingredients—we have the basics but you'll probably want more." He reached for a bowl, spooned a generous amount of beans and passed it to her. "If you're in Kara's schedule, you'll need the car to get to the hospital."

He picked up the second bowl he'd filled and the plate of corn bread, and indicated a breakfast table at one end of the large kitchen. "Is here okay with you?"

"Casual is good," she said, settling into the solid wooden chair. She tasted the chili beans and sighed. "It's possible that anything warm and home cooked would taste divine after a day of packing and traveling, but this is really good."

"We were raised eating Pamela's cooking." He glanced at the bread in his hand, a faraway look in his eyes. "It tastes like home to me."

They ate a few minutes in silence and the day's events played over in her mind.

"Can I ask you something?"

He glanced up, eyes wary. "Sure."

"Why does everyone sing Elvis songs to Flynn?"

A frown creased his forehead as he looked down at his bowl. "Grace was a big fan. She sang them to him instead of lullabies...."

"And now he asks for them," she finished for him.

"Yes."

It was one word, simply said, but it held an eternity of pain. It hurt to even watch so she tucked a stray piece of hair behind her ear and found a mischievous smile.

"I heard that not everyone sings them properly."

He glanced up sharply, his brilliant green eyes filled with confusion. "What do you mean?"

"He said that Aunty Lily sings her Elvis numbers too fast and occasionally dances to them, which is apparently inappropriate."

A reluctant smile tugged at the corners of his mouth. "That sounds like Lily."

And Daddy sings them sad.

The words pierced her heart. Of course he did—they reminded him of his beloved wife singing lullabies to their baby. It was amazing he could sing them at all. Unsure of what to say in the presence of so much grief, she ate another mouthful of chili.

"Susannah, there's something I want to ask of you, but..." Fine lines appeared around his eyes as pained reluctance overtook his face.

"Anything," she said softly. "Please, just ask and I'll do it." That's why she'd come. To help.

"It's not that kind of favor." He carefully placed his spoon in his bowl and steepled his hands together under his chin. "You'll be going home soon."

He paused so she said, "Yes," to fill the space.

"When I came back into the room this evening, and Flynn had fallen asleep, curled into your side..." He reached for his wine and had a mouthful, giving himself more time. "Flynn doesn't normally become affectionate with strangers, but he did with you for some reason, and if you spend more time with him—"

"You're worried that when I leave, he'll be hurt," she said, cutting in. She'd been tormented by the same thought.

"Basically." He picked up his spoon and stirred the food around his bowl before dropping the spoon back in and meeting her gaze. "I know I can't shelter him from every hurt, but if it's in my power to protect him, I will."

If only every child had a father who cared as much as Matthew. His love, his commitment to his son was etched in his every expression. "I promise I'll be careful when I spend time with him," she vowed. "I don't want to see him hurt, either."

"I know." There was certainty in his words, yet their time together today was the most they'd ever spent in each other's company—they were still virtually strangers.

So she couldn't help but ask, "You do?"

"I saw it in your eyes when you met him. You care."

She smoothed her skirt over her lap, gathering her thoughts—Matthew deserved to understand where she stood in regards to his son.

She looked back up and met his gaze. "When Flynn was handed to you and Grace at the maternity hospital, I was honestly pleased to be able to give you a baby. Grace was so desperate to be a mother, and I knew the two of you would make great parents. But, yes, I do still care about him. Want the best for him. So, please don't be concerned that I'll encourage an attachment that will hurt him when I leave."

A little of the tension seemed to leave his features as he nodded wordlessly and began to eat again.

After a few mouthfuls, the silence felt uncomfortable so she cast around for another topic.

"Do you have any allergies besides to penicillin?"

He arched an eyebrow and she realized she'd probably lost him by blurting out her question. "For when I buy ingredients tomorrow, I was wondering if you had a food allergy, like to peanuts or seafood," she added.

"I'm not fond of olives or oregano, but no, penicillin is my only allergy."

"It's tough that it might have stopped you from donating your bone marrow," she said without thinking, then cursed herself for reopening a painful subject.

A tortured look filled his eyes and she understood just how very much he'd wanted to be able to do that for his son. "Yes," he muttered.

The depths of pain she'd once again glimpsed called to her like a siren's song, demanding she ease the suffering.

"I'm sorry, Matthew."

He gave a small shrug. "I just wish I could be Flynn's first resort, not his last."

She wanted to ask how he was coping, but it was too intimate a question and she had no right to pry. He'd invited her into his home so she'd be nearby in case they needed her bone marrow. He didn't want her forming attachments to his son, or asking prying questions of him. She had to remember she was temporary. Nothing more.

Three

The next morning, Susannah was in the kitchen making toast when Matthew appeared, striding through the door, blowing her composure out the window. He wore trousers of darkest blue and a caramel business shirt—no jacket, no tie. The buttons at his neck and those leading down his chest weren't yet secured, giving an unfettered view of the strong column of his neck and his Adam's apple, then a glimpse of the smattering of dark chest hair. Her mouth suddenly went dry.

Until this morning, she'd seen his throat respectably outfitted in a collar and tie—even last night when he'd removed his tie, the collar had still covered the view now on display. Her heart thumped hard and erratically, which seemed an extreme reaction even considering this was the first time she'd seen his naked neck. Yet she couldn't tear her gaze away.

"Good morning, Susannah," he said, his voice smooth and deep. "Did you sleep well?"

She swallowed and determinedly looked back to the toaster. "Good morning. Yes, the room is lovely—I slept like a baby."

"You mean waking every two hours, feeling hungry?" She glanced back to see his green eyes had taken on a devilish glint.

The unexpected humor relaxed her and she smiled. "Flynn wasn't a good sleeper?"

"He was eight months before he slept through the night. But he's good now."

Matthew moved into the kitchen and reached toward a large silver machine. "I'm making coffee—do you want one?"

"Love one," she said on a happy sigh. She'd been eyeing the machine before he came down and wondering if she should attempt to work out how it operated, but was wary of breaking something on her first morning.

As she moved aside to give him more room, she noticed his feet were bare. Her breath caught. She'd seen plenty of naked male feet before—they were freely on show at any beach. But it was different seeing Matthew Kincaid's feet emerging from his suit trousers, moving around on his tiled kitchen floor. More intimate somehow. They were strong feet, broad with long toes and bluntly cut nails, and she had a vision of them sliding against her own feet. She shivered.

"How do you like yours?"

Her head jerked up to find him holding up a mug to highlight the question. His thoughts were innocent, it was hers that had been...best forgotten. That way lay danger.

"Black with one sugar," she rasped.

He pressed a button and a subtle mechanical noise filled the space between them, giving her a chance to recover her breath. Why was he affecting her so much? Was it the intense situation they faced? The false intimacy of staying in his house? Or something about Matthew Kincaid himself?

Abruptly the noise stopped and they were again two people standing in silence, alone in a kitchen.

"I'll make a proper breakfast tomorrow," she said, feigning normalcy, "but for today, do you want something other than toast?"

"Toast is fine. I usually make Flynn an omelet in the mornings but if I'm on my own, toast is all I bother with."

He leaned back against the counter, folding his arms over his muscled chest and crossing his naked feet at the ankles. She tried not to look as she slid two more pieces of bread into the toaster and moved to the fridge.

"Kara rang earlier," he said. "She wanted to know if you'd take the morning shift with Flynn. She was going to do it herself but there was some sort of wedding disaster she has to see to."

Delighted, she turned to him with butter in one hand and honey in the other. "She's getting married?" This family could do with something joyful to celebrate.

"Our sister Laurel is getting married. Kara is organizing the wedding. If it's a problem, I'll go. I'd planned on going into work this morning then spending the afternoon with Flynn, but—"

"It's no problem." She smiled, glad to be of use. "The only thing on my schedule was some shopping, and I'll do that later."

And the grateful smile that flashed across his face warmed her down to her toes and made any inconvenience worthwhile.

"Are you happy eating at the kitchen table?"

She glanced out through the glass doors to a little courtyard bathed in early morning sunlight. A wisp of serenity settled through her. "I saw a garden setting outside—would you mind if we ate out there?"

"Sure. It should be warm while the sun's hitting it," he said, walking over and unlocking the door. "In fact, it's been pretty warm this year."

She found a tray and piled it with plates, butter and spreads. Matthew put the coffees on the tray and leaned in front of her to lift it. The smell of clean skin and freshly laundered cotton surrounded her and her eyes drifted closed to savor the scent. When he moved away, her eyes flicked open again. Glad he hadn't seemed to have noticed, she grabbed some cutlery and followed him out onto the paved area that was warmed by the morning sun.

A light breeze played with the leaves on the bushy shrubs that enclosed the little courtyard. It was like a magical area, away from reality. Stepping away from the table, she turned her face to the sun, and, cutlery still grasped in one hand, spread her arms out to capture all the rays she could. The sunshine was so divine on her skin, the light breeze lovely as it lifted the edges of her hair, that she could have stayed for hours, soaking it all up. If she were alone.

She dropped her arms and turned to find Matthew standing a few feet away, watching her with an intensity that stole her breath. Telling herself there was no need to be self-conscious, she shrugged and laid the cutlery on the table.

"I like the fresh air," she said, a twinge of embarrassment still in her belly.

One corner of his mouth twitched. "I can see."

Ever since she was little, she'd searched out the sun and the wind, running outside on windy days to play. And now, as an adult, it was still something of a guilty pleasure.

"Working in an office all day and living in an apartment, I try to find time to be outside whenever I can. Just to feel the sun and the breeze touch my skin. It's...revitalizing."

The pulse at the base of his throat seemed to beat more strongly and his light tone was forced. "Sounds like a smart plan."

"I start to wilt if I stay inside too long," she said, aware her voice was breathier than it had been moments before.

A heavy silence fell, setting every nerve in her body on edge, until the tension drew out to become a physical thing between them. His eyes darkened, sending a shiver down her spine.

Finally he cleared his throat. "You're an interesting woman, Susannah Parrish."

"You don't like the outdoors?" Her uncooperative voice was close to a whisper.

"Love it," he said, stepping across to hold her chair for her. "I just never think of it as something I need. I take Flynn outside to play, and we go to parks, but it's something for him."

As she sank into the chair, she watched him move around the table to take his own seat. His tone had been matter-of-fact, but she sensed there was a clue here to understanding Matthew Kincaid. She picked up her coffee and sipped, turning the notion over in her mind.

"You can't live just for your work and Flynn. You have needs, too, Matthew."

He stilled, gaze locked on her and she suddenly regretted her choice of words—she had no right to be dishing out advice. She cast around for a way to make it right, to take the unintended provocative edge away, but came up with nothing.

His cell phone rang and he reached into his pocket, not breaking eye contact with her. Then he turned and headed for the glass door and into the house. "Matthew Kincaid," he said, closing the door behind him.

A trickle of relief flowed through her at the interruption. Though the courtyard was suddenly emptier, colder, without his presence. She rubbed her hands up and down her arms. In the short time since she'd arrived, she'd noticed that about him—he brought a room to life, as if there was a haze of…something… around him. Something almost magical. Even out here, outdoors, once he was gone, the air seemed flatter, the colors less vibrant.

The door opened and he reappeared. "That was the hospital."

Her heart skipped a beat. "Flynn?"

"No, it was the lab."

Her hands reached for the small table, and held firmly for support. "The tissue testing," she said and he nodded. "And?"

He grinned, and his face transformed. "They think you're a good match. It's the first piece of good news I've had since Flynn entered that hospital." He walked across to where she sat and took her hand, holding it between both of his. The touch of skin on skin was electric, sending a shimmer across every one of her nerve endings. "We finally have a backup plan, thanks to you."

"Oh, thank goodness," she said in a rush, partly from relief, partly from his hands still enclosing hers. She tightened her fingers around his.

"They're still not sure if he'll need it—" he dragged in a deep breath, and she could imagine the prayer he sent up "—but they'd like you to be available in case."

She didn't hesitate. "I've taken a week's leave. I'm yours."

Forty minutes later, she was entering Flynn's room, more nervous than she'd been yesterday. The first time she'd been alone with him, it'd been for a few minutes while Matthew made a call. This time, it would be several hours with a whole lot more expectation that she could be fun and entertaining. Which would be hard enough given her limited experience with children, but it also all needed to happen while not encouraging any attachment. She placed a hand over her belly to calm the butterflies that had taken up residence.

A tall woman with short, stylishly cut dark auburn hair hopped up from a chair against the wall and motioned with a finger against her lips that Flynn was sleeping while she tiptoed over. Her brilliant green eyes were the same shade as Matthew's, but she was too old to be a sister.

"You must be Susannah," the older woman said. "I'm Elizabeth, Flynn's grandmother. Thank you for filling in."

"It was no problem." As she turned and saw Flynn, her breath caught in her throat. His sweet little body was curled around the brown teddy, with the covers coming up to his waist. An almost physical pull beckoned her to his bedside, insisted she hold him.

The pull surprised her...and scared her. They'd been concerned about Flynn becoming attached to her—perhaps she should be as careful not to let herself become too emotionally involved with him, or risk breaking her own heart when she left.

"He's only been asleep for about ten minutes," Elizabeth said, "so he'll probably sleep a bit longer. It's hard to tell—he's tired all the time from the anemia so he'll probably want to nap a couple of times while you're here."

"I'll be fine." She spoke the words to Matthew's mother, but her gaze didn't waver from Flynn. "I'll let him set the pace, and I'll be sure to encourage him to rest if he seems tired."

"Kara said you were a friend of Grace's?" Elizabeth's tone was politely inquisitive, but Susannah understood her need to ask—this was a grandmother about to walk out and leave her only grandchild in the company of a stranger.

"Yes," she said, weighing up the amount of information to disclose. With a lie, it was best to stick as close to the truth as possible. "We knew each other a number of years ago. The last time I saw her was just after Flynn was born."

"You met Flynn?" the other woman asked, her head tilted to the side. "I'm sorry to sound so curious, it's just that I don't re-member you from the baby shower."

"Just the once." At his birth. "I missed the shower—I was moving to Georgia about that time, then Grace and I lost touch. I was very sorry to hear about her passing."

Elizabeth turned a pained look to her grandson. "We all were. For Grace, for Flynn and for Matthew." She reached for her bag and, while her face was averted, brushed at her cheek. Su-sannah's heart clenched tight for the pain this family had been through.

When Elizabeth straightened, her face was composed, even if her eyes glistened. "Nice to meet you, Susannah. I hope to run into you again sometime."

"Likewise," she replied, and watched Matthew's mother slip out of the room.

Now she was alone, Susannah allowed herself a chance to stare at the little boy for timeless, heart-wrenching minutes. He was simply perfect.

Finally she dragged herself away and eased into the chair. She rummaged through her bag for a pen and notebook then began making notes to email her assistant later. After her presentation yesterday, the PR plan for the bank's rebranding had been given the green light. She might have left soon after, but her assistant and the rest of the team could handle the preliminary work, and Susannah would be home long before the launch to take control of the rest of the plan. And she would stay in regular contact via phone and email.

She tapped the pen against her chin. A week ago, this project had been the most important thing in her life, and now...her gaze drifted over to the sleeping child before she forced it back again.

And now it still needed to be. She'd be leaving Charleston soon, and when she did, her career would again be her main focus. She loved her job, and was proud of being in a senior position at only twenty-six. She had a tight group of friends at home, too—she hadn't had a chance to explain her trip to Charleston to them yet, just a quick text to all four saying she was out of town and would explain when she got back. It was a good life she'd built when she and her mother had moved there three years ago. A life that anchored her and pulled at her to return.

When she'd finished making the notes, her mind drifted to dinner. She didn't regularly make elaborate meals, since it was just herself at home, but when she had an excuse, cooking was something she enjoyed. The only thing she knew about Matthew's tastes was he liked chili beans. Did he like desserts, or did he prefer a second helping of savory? Rich flavors or mild? She'd have to wing it the first time and see what worked for him. Ideas started to form and she jotted them down to make the trip to the supermarket easier.

Movement at the edge of her vision caught her attention. Flynn stretched and yawned then his large, sleepy eyes locked on her.

"Hello, sweetie," she said, moving to sit on the side of the bed. "Your grandma had to go, so I thought I might spend some time here." She was sure Elizabeth would have briefed him, but she wasn't sure how disoriented he'd be after waking.

He nodded. "Hello, Sudi."

Then, he leaned into her and yawned again. His little body was still warm from sleep and she wrapped him in a protective embrace and laid a cheek on his silky mop of hair.

Without meaning to, she turned her face and pressed her lips against the top of his head in a kiss. In that moment, she didn't want to let him go—he was so warm and soft and trusting in this just-woken state. She held the kiss a few seconds longer, wanting to create a memory—the feel of his small body, his scent. A memory she could carry with her forever.

When she released him, he pulled back and slowly blinked at her, curiosity in his eyes. "Are you my new mommy?"

Her heart stilled in her chest and she couldn't get her throat to work. Flynn seemed unaffected by her silence; he simply continued to watch her with soulful eyes.

"Why would you think that, sweetie?"

"You kiss like a mommy," he said matter-of-factly.

She drew in a shaky breath. "That's just the way I kiss all little boys and girls."

He didn't seem put off. "You singed like a mommy last time."

She opened her mouth, but what could she say? *Think fast.* "Maybe that just means I'll be someone else's mommy one day," she said brightly. "If I'm lucky, they'll be as wonderful as you."

He looked far from convinced, so she sat farther into the bed, dragging a leg up to sit sideways. She needed to address this head-on. "Here's the thing, Flynn. New mommies sometimes come along, but it's up to daddies to choose them."

He considered this before shaking his head. "I fink the kids should choose them."

"You have a point." She tried to suppress a smile—his argument had logic, but this could be a problem later and she needed to take it seriously. "You know, I don't really know much about how it works. But there *is* someone who knows."

"Who?" he asked, his eyes becoming impossibly big.

"Your dad. He's a smart man. I think you should ask him."

Flynn stared at her for a moment, and butterflies quivered in her stomach as she waited to see whether he would let her off the hook or not.

Then he got up on his knees, reached to the side table and retrieved the bear book they'd read yesterday. He passed it to her, eyes hopeful.

"I was just in the mood for a book about teddy bears," she said on a relieved breath.

He gave her a contented smile and curled into her side.

At lunchtime when Matt stepped into the anteroom to spend the afternoon with his son, Susannah was walking in to meet him from the other side. As she moved, her long blond hair swung around her shoulders and, though she was smiling, concern was clear in her eyes.

He mirrored her smile as she slipped through the door in case Flynn was watching. "Is something wrong?"

"Nothing new about his condition." She paused and bit down on her lip and his eyes were drawn to the action. Such a plump lip, tailor-made for the nibbling it was currently having. He turned away. He shouldn't be thinking about Susannah Parrish's lip.

"But I wanted to forewarn you about a question you'll probably get."

Relief flowed through him, and he bent to wash his hands. "He's always been challenging with his questions."

"Flynn asked if I was his new mommy."

He snapped to attention and pivoted to face her, hands dripping on the floor. "How did that come up?"

"I swear, Matthew," she said, wrapping her arms around her middle, "I didn't encourage him."

That was true—Susannah could never cause anyone pain on

purpose, he knew that deep in his bones. He tapped the faucet off with his elbows and reached for a paper towel.

"I know." He threw the towel in the bin and took a breath. "But do you know where he got the idea?"

Her eyes flicked to Flynn through the window. "He says I kiss like a mommy, and sing like one, too."

He winced. Strong pieces of evidence to a three-year-old. "What did you tell him?"

"I said daddies were the ones to choose the new mommies and he should talk to you about it." Although her eyes were still worried, a grin peeped out. "He thinks kids should choose the new mommies."

Matt couldn't restrain a chuckle. "That sounds like our Flynn. Thanks for aiming him back to me—I'll handle it from here."

Not that he had any idea what he'd say to the kid who was too wise for his own good. As much as Matt had tried to protect him when Grace died, his son had changed. Now he saw too much. Thought too much.

And he deserved better than a father who was making it up as he went along. Grace had been the one who'd always known what to do with kids. Even when they'd been talking about a divorce, he'd still expected they would share custody afterward.

Now he was all Flynn had. He looked through the glass panel at his son flicking through his favorite teddy-bear book.

He would just have to do better.

Four

Susannah watched Matthew eat the last spoonful of her coffee and hazelnut cheesecake. A warm glow suffused her body when he made an appreciative sound. Cooking calmed her—somehow allowed her thoughts to fall into order—so she would have wanted to cook today regardless. But to have someone enthusiastically appreciate her food made it that bit more worthwhile. Especially when that someone was Matthew, whose opinion she'd come to respect.

"After a meal like that, I don't think you need to worry about pulling your weight," he said, leaning back into his chair and giving her a lazy appraisal.

"It's one of my mom's many recipes." Her mother had taught her to cook from when she was young—savory meals, desserts, cakes. They'd been the recipes her own mother had taught her, and maybe one day Susannah would have her own little girl or boy to teach them to. A picture of Flynn flashed in her mind, but she pushed it away. He was *Matthew's* son, not hers.

"I can see that you and your father ate well."

"My dad passed away when I was young, so it was mainly Mom and me." The familiar ache swelled to fill her chest. It'd been many years but she still missed her father immeasurably, missed his hugs, his radiant love for her mother and her.

"I'm sorry to hear that," he said, genuine concern in the fine lines around his eyes. "I lost my father not long ago."

Headlines in the local newspaper had screamed the new developments in the story to passersby when she'd been at the store earlier. She'd picked up a copy and read the first few lines about Reginald Kincaid's murder, then placed the paper back on the pile and moved on, unwilling to be another vulture, prying for details of something so intensely private.

For the rest of the afternoon, she hadn't been able to stop thinking about the story, her heart aching for Matthew. So much grief and burden—first his wife's tragic death and becoming a single parent to Flynn. Now losing his father, and discovering it was through murder.

The urge to reach out and touch his hand verged on irresistible—had there been anyone to comfort him? His wife was gone and each family member would have been suffering their own grief. She glanced at his broad shoulders, his strong frame. What would it be like, drawing him close and offering a consoling embrace? Her skin warmed. Probably less about giving comfort and more about her fascination with him, judging by her body's response to the mere thought.

She settled for wrapping her fingers around her wineglass. "Were you and your father close?"

He nodded once, his lips curving into a grim smile. "We're a close family." A frown line appeared on his forehead then grew while he studied his empty plate. "Well, I thought we were."

She remembered the obvious affection between Matthew and Kara, and the way he'd spoken about his other siblings. "What's made you question it?"

His gaze was on his empty plate but she knew he didn't see it. Even as he spoke, she knew his focus was a million miles away.

"After my father's death," he said through a tight jaw, "we discovered he had a second family. Complete with two extra sons—one biological and one informally adopted. Seems that, decades ago, he met up again with his first love to find she'd borne him a son, been married and had another son to her husband. By the time she met Dad again, the husband was gone, so Dad set her up as his mistress and created a second family for himself with her and the boys."

She leaned back in her chair, physically rocked by the revelation, despite not knowing his father. The betrayal, the anger, must have been overwhelming.

"You had no idea?" she whispered.

His eyes were bleak. "None at all."

"Oh, Matthew, I can't imagine how awful that must have been. Especially to find out that way."

"It was no picnic," he said and reached for his wineglass before taking a long sip.

"So, beyond the shock, is it a good thing getting two new brothers?"

He dragged a hand down his face. "I don't think the new brothers are looking to play happy families. Jack, my father's biological son, definitely isn't and the jury's still out on Alan. Also, the way my father divided the stock between both groups has left the family company in a precarious position."

"I'm so sorry. Sometimes life is simply unfair."

He gave her an ambiguous smile and stood to clear the plates. "Tell me about your mother."

She recognized the change of topic for what it was—he'd exposed too much for comfort to a virtual stranger—so she allowed him the preservation of his dignity.

"My mother is fun," she said and followed him to the sink with their wineglasses. "Always lively, always ready with a witty joke. It must have been hard for her after my father died, but she rarely let on."

He opened the dishwasher and looked up, genuine curiosity in his eyes before he stacked their crockery in the slots. "How old were you when he died?"

"Eight." She had no clear memories left of that time, just the overwhelming sense of sadness and despair. Poor Flynn must have experienced similar depths after losing Grace, and she wished with everything inside her she could have saved him that. At least he had Matthew, the way she had her mother.

"My parents were very much in love," she said, "but Mom pulled herself together quickly to ensure my world was stable. I see you've done the same thing for Flynn and I really respect that."

A quick grimace passed across his face before he turned away to grab a cooking pot. "Did you have much family around?" he asked.

"Mom's parents were interstate and they'd help where they could. Dad's parents were less helpful." The resentment that lived in the pit of her stomach threatened to simmer, but she wouldn't let it. She wouldn't let them ruin her mood all this time later.

He straightened and his green gaze narrowed on her. "Define 'less helpful.'"

Perceptive man, Matthew Kincaid. For an instant, she considered deflecting the question, or giving a half response, but he'd just shared a very personal story and she couldn't be less than honest in return.

"They sued for custody of me after Dad died."

Very slowly, he put the cutlery down and rested his hands low on his hips. "Were there any grounds?"

"Only in their imaginations. They'd never liked or approved of my mother. She was an outsider to their social scene. My father had provided a buffer for her when he was alive, but once he was gone, they pulled out all the stops."

Her father's family had money and influence—a lethal combination. It had taught her young that wealthy families who were used to getting their own way were dangerous. Her mother had been blinded by love when she'd married, but Susannah had learned from that mistake. Families like her father's—like the Kincaids—were full of secrets and maneuverings. She'd bet the Kincaids had a few more secrets up their sleeves, too. Families like theirs always did.

"Criminal," Matthew said, scowling. "To make it harder for you both while you were grieving is unforgivable."

The unqualified support loosened the knot in her chest where the memory lived and allowed a little more of the story to ease out. "Not just while we were grieving. When they lost the custody case, they wiped Mom. Wouldn't acknowledge she existed. Mom would drop me over on visits once a month, and they'd shower me with presents and try to convince me to live with them."

"I can't imagine Grace's parents doing something that selfish. They adore Flynn—they stay with us regularly, and ring him every Sunday. Thinking of them pulling Flynn away from me...it's just inconceivable." He shook his head. "Did you tell your mother?"

"No, I just put up with it." Until they went too far.

"How are they now?" he asked with a raised eyebrow, obviously being far too perceptive once again.

She hesitated before admitting, "I wouldn't know."

"You stood up to them," he said, warm approval in his eyes. "What was the tipping point?"

It was a time in her life that she avoided revisiting, and had never told anyone else about, yet, it seemed somehow natural to share with this man.

"Four years ago," she began, then moistened her lips, "my mother lost everything in a despicable scam. She'd trusted someone she worked with who disappeared after the scam went down. Lots of people were stung and despite the authorities being called in, there was no chance of recovering her money. She was going to lose the house she'd shared with my father. Her family didn't have a lot of money, so she made me promise not to tell them. But my father's family was rich, and she was their daughter-in-law."

"She didn't know you asked, did she?"

She shook her head.

"What did they say?"

"They were exquisitely polite and very sorry not to be able to help, but—" she flinched, remembering their falsely sympathetic faces "—the bottom line was they wouldn't spend the money on a woman they didn't care for and had never wanted in their family."

She'd learned something that day—something she'd already known but had been trying to avoid admitting. Wealth changed people. Especially families. When money was inherited, it changed the family dynamics. Made life into an "us and them" scenario. She wanted enough money to get by, but huge wealth wasn't something she wanted anything to do with. And she'd never marry into a rich family the way her mother had.

He moved forward the smallest of steps and ran his fingertips down her arm in a gesture that was comforting even as it made her pulse jump.

"Susannah, I'm sorry." His voice was deep with concern.

"One good thing came of it," she said, trying to ignore the fingers that now rested near her elbow. "I went home, legally changed my name to my mother's maiden name and haven't seen them since."

If she'd lost her father's name in the process, that was regrettable but ultimately it was okay—her father had hated the way his parents had treated his wife, so she knew he would have understood. And she had him living in her heart, which was more important than a name.

"Good for you." One corner of his mouth kicked up. "So what happened with your mother?"

"I took out a loan for as much as I could get approved, and I met Grace soon after. Your money for the surrogacy paid the balance on Mom's house. It's rented out for the time being to help with loan repayments, and we moved to Georgia so Mom could live with family till the bank is paid out."

His fingertips began to trace a pattern on her skin once more, causing her pulse to jump erratically. "The house was that important?"

"She'd worked her entire life and," she said around a tight ball of emotion in her throat, "after Dad died she worked two jobs to give me the best start in life she could manage. I couldn't let her lose her house, the home for her retirement, her one link back to the man she loved."

With sure hands, he pulled her into his arms. She resisted at first, she was used to dealing with things on her own and she'd only known this man a couple of days, but he held her with a gentle firmness until she relaxed into his warmth. He was offering his support so freely, and just this once, she allowed herself to simply absorb.

And yet, there was something else that thrummed between them, a dangerous craving that always seemed to be lurking just beneath the surface when they were together.

She knew she should move away, banish the craving.

But she didn't.

Lately Matt wasn't used to having any woman in his arms besides his mother or his sisters. Susannah Parrish didn't feel remotely like his sisters. Her eyes, filled with strength and hurt at the betrayal had been his undoing. He couldn't have stood another second with the distance between them. And, even though he rubbed a palm slowly up and down her back the way he might for Lily, Laurel or Kara, he couldn't begin to fool himself.

This wasn't platonic—her nearness was setting his skin on fire.

He'd never known why she'd carried his baby, what she'd

used the money for, but the story of her resilience was amazing. Could he have ever done something as difficult for similar reasons?

"If I'd known, we'd have paid you more." Heck, if he thought she'd take it, he'd give her more now.

"It was enough," she said softly. "But thank you for saying that."

"What if I give—"

She pulled back in his arms and he could see her face again. "Please don't offer. I'll be fine."

"Noble as well as generous and beautiful," he said, cupping her cheek in his hand. Her pupils dilated and her breath came faster, and he wanted to kiss her so badly that he ached with it. He leaned down, wanting...

"Matthew," she said, and he stopped close enough to feel her breath on his face as she spoke. "This isn't a good idea."

"It sure feels like a good idea," he said, not retreating an inch. And, God help him, at this moment he couldn't consider anything other than how her mouth would feel opening beneath his.

"Things," she began, then paused to swallow. "Things are too complicated already."

"It's just a kiss, Susannah," he told her...told himself. "It doesn't have to mean anything." He brushed his lips across hers lightly, needing to feel them. "Just—" over one corner of her mouth "—one—" then the other corner "—kiss."

On a sigh, her lips parted, and a shudder ripped through his body. He'd been trying to deny that he'd wanted her ever since she'd walked through the arrivals gate at the airport. In the past year, any flicker of desire—no matter how minor—had felt disloyal to Grace, and had been followed by a tidal wave of guilt. Despite the talks of divorce, they'd still been married when she'd died. Worse, if he hadn't suggested divorce in the first place, Grace would still be alive. The confusion had kept him closed to the idea of other women for twelve months.

But what Susannah stirred within him was too strong to deny.

Her mouth tasted of the sweet dessert, combined with an allure all of her own that drew him ever deeper.

He plowed his fingers through her silken hair, holding her for his kiss, unwilling to risk her withdrawal. The wet slide of her tongue against his was sinfully erotic, her teeth nibbling at his lip explosive.

Mindless, he found her hips and drew her closer. As close as he could get while clothes provided a barrier. Her hands skimmed over his shoulders and down his back, and he wanted nothing more than to feel those hands on bare skin. To have his hands on her bare skin. He wanted her with an all-consuming need that was beyond thought.

He reached for the first button on her blouse but before he could make any headway, she pulled back.

"Matthew," she rasped, resting her hands on his chest. "Please."

The rough edges in her voice reverberated through his body. "Please, what?" he asked with a smile.

"If you try to kiss me like that again—" she paused, as if gathering enough breath to continue "—I won't be able to resist."

His pulse leaped. "Good," he said and his head began a descent again.

"Flynn." The one word was all she said, but it broke through the sensual fog in his brain and he paused.

"What about Flynn?"

She stepped beyond the circle of his arms, and his hand drifted down from her shoulder, lingered at her elbow then, when he reached her hand, his fingers tangled with hers. She looked at their entwined fingers for so long he wondered if she would say anything. Then she looked up, and sucked her bottom lip into her mouth. Barely a minute ago, she'd done the same thing to his lip and this time, he wanted to drag hers into his own mouth. But he waited, holding himself in check until he could kiss her again.

"When I was young," she finally said, leaning back against the counter, "and my grandparents would ask me to live with them, they'd tell me it was what my father would have wanted. I missed him terribly and they used that to get what they wanted. I know this is a completely different situation, but I've never forgotten that feeling of being torn. Of the confusion."

He squeezed his eyes shut and held them closed as he tried to get his brain to follow the quick change from kissing her to talking about her childhood. Was she seriously thinking Flynn was at risk—from her?

He cocked his head to the side. "You'd never do something that despicable to Flynn."

"Never," she confirmed with a fierceness in her expression. "But I truly believe we need to keep the family arrangements clear so Flynn doesn't sense any confusion and read into it that he's getting a new mommy. He's very astute."

Matt released her fingers and scrubbed his hands through his hair. She was right—Flynn was very perceptive for his age. Some of the things that came out of that kid's mouth astounded him. And with all the upheavals in his family at the moment, following his grandfather's death, and two new "uncles" he hadn't yet met arriving on the scene, the last thing Flynn needed was any more uncertainty. He'd already asked if Susannah was his new mommy.

"All right." He blew out a long breath. "There's some chemistry between us, we can't deny that." In fact, it was baffling that he felt this strongly about someone he barely knew, but there was no ignoring anymore that he did. "Perhaps it would be better all-around if we didn't take it further."

"Yes," she whispered, watching his mouth. His skin heated.

"And if we're going to ignore it, it'd help enormously if you didn't look at me that way. I only have the willpower of one man."

Her gaze flicked to her feet and she shuffled back. "I'm sorry."

With a finger, he lifted her chin until he could see her eyes again. "Don't be sorry." Gently he smoothed her hair back from her face. "We won't act on this, but promise you'll never feel sorry for wanting me."

"Okay," she said, her voice tight.

"And I won't be sorry for wanting you," he said roughly then left the room before he forgot his promise and kissed her.

Matt stood in the anteroom to his son's hospital bedroom, washing his hands and watching Susannah. Flynn was asleep and she was curled in the visitor's chair, reading a book—her legs tucked beneath her, her hair falling forward to curtain her face. The air caught in his chest. Everything inside him demanded he finish what they'd started last night. But she'd been right to stop their kiss—it had been a monumentally stupid move on his part. As if things weren't already messy enough with keeping the secret about Flynn's biological mother from his family, and ensuring stability and clarity for Flynn.

And Grace had been so jealous of Susannah during the pregnancy—not only was she carrying their baby, but the baby was biologically a product of him and Susannah. How much worse would Grace have felt if she'd known he'd soon be lusting over Susannah? After creating the situation that had killed his wife, the very last person he should be thinking of bedding was Susannah Parrish.

So why was his body convinced otherwise? Annoyed with himself, he shook the water from his hands with a bit too much force, and turned to grab a paper towel. As he did, he caught sight of a man coming through the door. A man who made Matthew's fingers curl into fists.

Jack Sinclair.

His father's oldest child. The man their father had left forty-five percent of The Kincaid Group to in his will and who had made his dislike of his father's legitimate family abundantly clear. Jack had been playing his cards close to his chest so far, but no one doubted his intentions—to take over TKG and fold it into his own company, Carolina Shipping.

With frustration and resentment fueling his scowl, Matt thrust his hands on his hips. "What the heck makes you think you'd be welcome here?"

Jack met the glare with one of his own, feet solidly planted shoulder width apart. "Regardless of how we feel about each other, that little boy is my nephew. I spent a couple of months in the hospital myself when I was a child and I intend to see him."

A touch of humanity from the enemy…or a ploy? "I notice you didn't bother to call first."

"Would you have invited me to visit if I had?"

Before Matt could reply, the door opened again and a third man entered the room, completing the bizarre triangle of Reginald Kincaid's sons—Matt's brother RJ.

RJ froze midstride, looking from one man to the other before his furious gaze settled on Matt. "What the hell is he doing here?"

Matt was heartened by the support of his brother's outrage. "I was just asking the same thing."

As one, the brothers turned to face the interloper.

Jack rolled his shoulders back and held up a gift bag. "I've brought a toy. I'm a blood relation to the boy and I want to meet him."

The door to Flynn's room slid open and Susannah slipped through. Just seeing her face made a large chunk of Matt's stress evaporate, replaced by a tugging desire deep in his gut. Unable to help himself, he moved to her side and placed a hand at the small of her back, trying to ensure it appeared platonic, but feeling uncomfortably proprietorial in a room of three men.

"Susannah, this is my brother RJ. Susannah is an old friend of Grace's who's been visiting Flynn."

RJ leaned over to shake her hand, taking his gaze from Jack long enough to smile at her. "Nice to meet you, ma'am."

"Likewise," Susannah said.

Matt glanced up at Jack and narrowed his eyes. "And this is Jack Sinclair. My father's other son."

Susannah shook Jack's proffered hand. "Nice to meet you, Jack," she said, then faced down each man in turn. "I know you've both just met me, so this might seem out of line, but there's so much tension in this room, it's ready to smother me. And Flynn will feel it, too. You can't all go into his room together."

There was something of a mother lion in her eyes, and Matt knew that if his brothers tried to walk in, she wouldn't be afraid to stand in their way. His chest swelled. It was a beautiful thing to watch.

Jack again held his gift bag aloft. "I'd like to give this to the boy."

Susannah glanced over, raising her eyebrow the barest hint, yet he understood—she was asking if he'd let her take Jack in to Flynn's room, alone. He glanced over at Flynn through the glass wall—he was watching the interaction. If he tried to eject Jack, Flynn would see, and Matt would do anything to keep Flynn's world stable at the moment. No confrontations, no ripples in the pond.

And he had to admit, no matter how much it galled, this man was a blood relation to Flynn. Though why that would mean anything to Jack Sinclair, he had no idea.

He relaxed his body language for Flynn's sake, but he glared at his half brother with all the animosity inside. "This is a one-time deal, Sinclair. You go in, you give him the present, you leave again. And you don't come back."

Jack glared back and spoke through a tight jaw. "Understood."

He silently nodded to Susannah—she was right that they couldn't all go in together. The best environment for Flynn would be if Jack went with her. While she explained the gown and hand-washing routine to Jack, Matt steered RJ out into the hall.

He planted himself in front of the glass panel in the wall—
he might have given the okay for Jack to go in, but at the first
sign that Flynn was even slightly uncomfortable or unhappy,
he'd throw the gate-crasher out himself.

"So, how is the little tyke?" RJ asked, concern clear in his
voice.

"His blood work is a little better." He'd caught the doctor on
the way in and heard the latest scores. Flynn wasn't out of the
woods by any means, but any improvement, however small, was
good news. It meant needing a bone-marrow transplant was less
likely, and brought the day he could come home that bit closer.

"I can't tell you how glad I am," RJ said, clapping Matt on
the back. "Let's hope it continues that way."

Matt allowed himself half a smile at the prospect. Unwilling to jinx it, he didn't want to dwell on Flynn's improvements
too much—the blood work had improved before…then dived
again. But his brother's enthusiasm allowed him the space for
just a moment to consider that his little boy's health was really
on the mend.

They watched Jack enter Flynn's room and Susannah perform
the introductions and the atmosphere in the corridor changed.
From the corner of his eye, he could see RJ mirroring his battle
stance of straight back, hands low on hips and—he knew without looking—a scowl.

"Any news on who owns the last ten percent?" Matt asked.
Their father had left forty-five percent of The Kincaid Group to
be shared among his legitimate children, and another forty-five
percent to Jack Sinclair. No one knew where the last ten percent
was—the ownership had been hard to trace past the shares being
sold to a now-defunct business—but they needed them fast.

Anger at his father burned in his gut—both for keeping his
second family a secret and for giving Jack shares in the family
company which had led to this predicament. Their father had
left them a letter each, which most of them had opened at the
will reading, hoping for an explanation of his actions. As far as

he was aware, none of them had got one. Matt hadn't wanted to even touch his letter, let alone open it. Had his father stood in front of him that day, Matt would have turned and walked away. And the rage still seethed down deep. The last thing he wanted was to speak to a man who'd kept such monstrous secrets, had betrayed them so badly, even if it was only via a letter. Barely resisting crumpling the envelope and tossing it, he'd thrown it in a desk drawer in the unlikely event he changed his mind. He should have burnt it.

But he had to shove the emotions aside and strategize if they were to succeed. RJ was acting CEO, and Laurel, Kara, Lily and he would vote with RJ to install RJ as permanent CEO, but they needed the ten percent to outvote Jack if—when—he opposed. Until then, they were stuck in a stalemate.

"No news." RJ blew out a disgusted breath. "But I've put Nikki Thomas on the case. She's vowed to have the owner present when we vote."

"If anyone will find them, Nikki will." Their father had hired the corporate investigator not long before he died, and she'd managed to impress them already with her determination and ability to get results.

"Jack's given nothing away?" Matt asked. "I wouldn't put it past him to have located the shares and bought them already."

RJ shook his head. "He's playing his cards close to his chest, so if he has them, he wouldn't be sharing the information with us. He's a cold one. He'll be planning even now to get the ten percent and fold TKG into his own company."

Matt winced, but he'd had that exact thought himself. "What about Alan—any chance he's got them?" It seemed their father had taken his mistress's other son under his wing somewhat, yet not left him any stock in the will.

"I doubt it. If Dad had wanted to give him stock, it would have been at the same time as the rest of us. Though I have been thinking about Alan."

Through the glass panel, Matt surveyed Jack awkwardly

trying to make conversation with Flynn. "Alan seems like the better man of the two."

RJ grunted his agreement. "I'm wondering if Alan will want a job. At the next board meeting, Jack could use his shares to demand we employ his brother."

"Alan said he was between jobs, so he might want something," Matt said.

"And I don't think Jack will settle for a mere job. He's got his eye on the prize. Everything."

A lead weight dropped into his stomach as he acknowledged the truth in that. They stared at the scene through the glass panel for another couple of minutes as Jack awkwardly handed the gift bag over toward Flynn, who tentatively took it, one hand holding Susannah's fingers.

"One thing I can promise you," RJ said, "I won't let that man ruin TKG."

There was a fierceness in RJ's voice that was unusual. Matt turned to study his brother's face. The whole family had been thrown off balance, not only by their father's death, but the revelations about his second family, then the forty-five percent of company stock being willed to Jack. Even so, RJ had always been easygoing, even when he was in corporate shark mode.

He was about to ask what was going on, but inside Flynn's room, Jack moved to the door, and Matt needed to get inside to hold his son and make sure he was all right after meeting his new uncle. And he needed to see Susannah, to thank her for intervening, to ensure she was okay, as well. Analyzing RJ's mood change could wait.

Five

Five days later, Susannah was wandering the aisles of Matthew's basement wine cellar. Flynn had shown some definite improvement, but he wasn't yet past the risk that he might need the bone-marrow transplant, so she'd extended her leave for another week.

As the days had drifted on, she'd taken to slipping down to Matthew's wine cellar a few times a day for respite from the house—it was the only room that wasn't dominated by Grace's presence. Which was appropriate—this was Grace's house—and she hated herself for feeling a little jealous.

Down here it was shadowy and cool and strongly masculine. The shelving was made of dark wood, in straight lines and sharp angles.

She held a warm mug of tea between her hands as she perused the labels. Möet. Dom Pérignon. Krug. Veuve Clicquot.

"Thinking of taking up wine collecting?" The voice that caught her off guard was deep and smooth and faintly amused.

She turned to find Matthew casually leaning on the door frame, ankles crossed, hands deep in pockets.

Her heart turned over in her chest. It was a strange thing— she'd dated men before, had even flirted with the idea of marriage with one long-term boyfriend. But no man, boyfriend or otherwise, had ever affected her the way Matthew Kincaid could. All without a touch—he stood eight feet from her, but the heat of his gaze made her skin tighten. Made her want his kiss with a desperation that was alien to her.

She swallowed and found her voice. "How long have you been standing there?"

"Long enough to see how relaxed you are, perusing my collection." He pushed off the door frame and prowled toward her. "This isn't your first time in here, is it?"

An electric shiver raced up her spine. "Would you prefer I didn't come down?"

"You're welcome to explore any part of the house and grounds." He stopped within touching distance, his face in shadow, but she could hear that his breathing was a touch more rapid than normal. "I'm just interested why you chose a cellar over, say, the conservatory."

His nearness set off a series of pinprick sparks throughout her body. She rubbed her forearms, attempting to dispel the sensation, but it made no difference.

"Normally I would, but...things seem simpler down here," she said, attempting to explain what she only barely understood herself. "Clearer."

He turned and the muted light caught the planes of his face, making him look stark. Dangerous. Desirable.

"You're looking for simplicity?" he asked, voice low.

"Aren't you?"

He watched her mouth as he spoke. "I guess I am."

"And things between us would never be simple."

"Maybe not," he drawled, "but they'd be good."

A shiver of gooseflesh raced across her skin. Instinctively she knew it was the truth. That making love with Matthew Kincaid would be an exquisite experience. It had been in his kiss. It was in his heated gaze. It was in his slow, deliberate step closer.

"We agreed we wouldn't act on this," she said, her voice wavering.

He stopped mere inches from her, his Adam's apple bobbing slowly down then up. "We were stupid."

"We were thinking of Flynn," she said, trying to sound sure. "That he needs to know exactly where everyone fits in his life. No place for confusion."

He ran a finger down the side of her face. "He's not here. He's with Lily, probably playing games the nurses wouldn't approve of, if I know my sister."

The temptation was so strong, it was a physical force, drawing her ever closer into the magical aura that surrounded him. His lips—so close—beckoned. Their kiss had been playing on an unending replay loop for five days, driving her to distraction, reminding her of the delicious pressure of his mouth, the smooth eroticism of his tongue meeting hers. If she simply leaned forward, she could taste the pleasure again.

But the other image that had been replaying in her mind was Flynn's solemn, hopeful eyes when he'd asked if she was his new mommy. Each time she remembered, it broke her heart anew.

"If I come with you to your bed right now—" his eyes flared and she steeled herself against the allure "—we'd change in our interactions with each other afterward. Flynn doesn't *have* to be here now...he'll see us together later. He'll know something's changed."

His eyes drifted closed and squeezed tight, as if against a blow, before slowly opening again. "And he's already watching you too closely for comfort."

"I'm the last woman you can afford to get involved with."

There was silence for a heartbeat, two. Then he closed his eyes again and took a step back. "It's a shame you think ahead."

"A curse of working in public relations."

"Since we can only do things that are above reproach, would you like to help me choose a bottle of wine for dinner?"

She glanced around. "I don't know anything about wine."

"I'll teach you," he said, his voice too deep and smooth for a conversation about beverages. With a hand lightly resting on her waist, he guided her to another row. "You were in the champagne section. This is the first of the reds." He picked out a bottle and handed it to her. "That's a 1929 Burgundy."

Suddenly realizing the bottle must be worth a small fortune, she handed it back. "Are they all old bottles?"

"I'm more interested in drinking the wine than keeping it, but I do have a few, like this one, that are worth holding on to." He replaced it and they moved down the row before he pulled out another bottle. "This is a 2004 Pinot Noir. One of my favorites, so I pick up a few bottles wherever I see them." He shrugged one shoulder as if they were talking about collecting items no more expensive than her tea mug. "What do you usually drink?"

"If I'm at a restaurant, I follow the waiter's suggestions of what wine will go with the meal."

"We can do that. Tell me what was that heavenly scent that hit me when I walked in the door?"

"Crème brûlée for tonight." Her favorite—rich, creamy and decadent.

"Then I suggest—" he guided her several rows away with that heated palm at her lower back "—we open a dessert wine after the main meal." He scanned the rows before gently pulling out a dark, dusty bottle. "Perhaps this one."

As she took the bottle, she looked blindly at the label, but instead of reading, her full attention was on the aftershave that wrapped around her like a cloak, and under that, the scent of Matthew himself, robbing her of logical thought. He took the bottle from her hands and she focused on the action like a beacon, bringing her back to reality.

She moistened her lips. "Do you normally have wine with your dessert?"

"I don't usually have dessert," he said beside her ear, "but it's fast becoming my favorite time of day."

Before she could process the words, he turned and strode to a shelf along the wall that held an assortment of items and retrieved a bottle opener. She watched his strong hands work quickly and smoothly as he screwed the gadget into the cork, then eased the cork out. The man's hands were a work of art. How would they feel on her body...? The air around her thickened, becoming harder to draw into her lungs.

He replaced the bottle opener on the shelf and picked up a tasting glass. She watched, mesmerized, as he poured a small amount into the glass, swirled it a few times, then passed it to her.

"Taste," he softly commanded.

She took the glass and raised it to her lips. "It's sweet."

"Very," he agreed, his gaze on her mouth.

She tipped the glass and the wine flowed over her tongue, rich and sweet, with a depth of flavor. A small purr of approval escaped her throat.

"Now imagine you've had a spoonful of the crème brûlée first, and then sipped this."

She closed her eyes and focused on the flavors and how they would combine and the effect was positively sinful. Then other decadent images flooded into her mind—Matthew's powerfully built body stretched out before her on his bed; the feel of him pressed against her in passion; the sound he'd make when he found release....

As her eyes flicked open, she found him watching her, unblinking, his pupils large in his brilliant green eyes. More than anything, she wanted to lean into his strength, to take him up on the promise his eyes held. But there had been a reason not to do that—for the life of her, she couldn't think of it right now, but she was sure there had been one earlier.

"I—I—" She paused to gain control over the stammer that had suddenly appeared in her voice. "I'd better check on the dessert in the oven—it'd be a shame to ruin it now we have a wine to match it."

"Yes," he agreed, his voice like gravel. "You should check on that."

She turned and flew up the stairs to the safety of the kitchen, hoping like all hell that Matthew didn't follow her until her equilibrium had time to reestablish itself. And until she remembered that reason she couldn't crawl into his bed.

Matthew had suffered through the sumptuous dinner, trying to keep his growing fascination for Susannah under control. Yet he hadn't been able to avoid noticing every time her fork passed between her lips, every movement her creamy throat made as she swallowed. And as she'd walked across the kitchen to serve the dessert, the gentle sway of her hips had his skin tightening. Every night he came home to this torture and it was getting worse each time.

"I'll pour the wine." Desperate to find something for his hands to do, he pushed to his feet and grabbed the bottle of dessert wine he'd brought up from the wine cellar earlier.

The change was no improvement to his circumstances. He had to retrieve glasses, which were in a cupboard beside her. As he opened the door and curled his hands around two glasses, a sweet fragrance enveloped him and he stilled to breathe it more fully. Floral, perhaps jasmine. Maybe gardenia.

With a start, he realized he was standing beside her with his hand in an open cupboard and she was looking at him curiously. Her lips were slightly parted and he remembered tasting them as if it had been mere moments ago.

"I was going to serve the crème brûlée with whipped cream on the side," she said, her voice uncertain, as if filling the silence.

"Sounds good."

Roughly grabbing the bottle, he stalked across the room, and poured the wine. He had to stop obsessing about Susannah Parrish. Surely her effect on him was merely proximity? Being in his house, sleeping down the hall, making herself at home in his kitchen. Beside his family and his personal assistant, he hadn't spent this much time with any woman since Grace's death.

Whatever it was, it was purely physical. He would never develop any stronger feelings for a woman again. Wasn't sure he was even capable of it. But desire? Oh, yeah. He was sure capable of that right now. And then some.

She reached in front of him to lay his plate on the table, and he tracked the progress of her arm—the skin was smooth and pale, and he was certain it would feel soft. Luxuriant. Then, at the last moment, as she released the plate, he saw her hand tremble. He raked his gaze over her, noticing every detail and realized she held a tension in her body that matched his own. A flush spread from her neck down till it disappeared under her blouse.

He held back a curse. This would be so much easier to ignore if it was an unrequited desire.

She sank into her seat and gave him a tentative smile, and all he could do was offer a tight nod in return before sampling her brûlée.

The first taste slid over his tongue with wicked richness and he almost groaned. It was sex on a spoon. He glanced up at Susannah—did it have the same effect on her?—but her eyes were studiously focused on her plate as she ate.

Perversely wanting her to react, wanting to see if she was in the same hell he'd been condemned to, he lifted his glass. "Try the wine. It'll bring out the flavors."

She glanced up, her tongue darting out to lick a speck of sticky golden dessert from her bottom lip and the blood drained from his head. She lifted the glass and sipped, then took another spoonful into her mouth, and it was as if a cloud of bliss enveloped her. Her pupils dilated and her skin glowed.

He wanted that. Wanted to see her entire body reaching for nirvana.

With him deep inside her.

He held back the harshest oath he could think of and shoved the plate away. "You have a talent."

With skepticism clear in her gaze, she looked from the plate to his eyes. "Yet you didn't finish it."

"I'll have it later. I need to go for a run." If he pushed his body to the point of exhaustion, maybe he'd get some relief from the relentless need for her. There were shoes and running clothes in the car, he'd grab them on the way out. He stood and took his plate to the sink, heart thundering, then gripped the edges of the counter, summoning the strength to walk out the door.

"You've just eaten a full meal and you want to go for a run?" The soft voice came from behind him.

Unable to look at her, he focused on the shadowy trees out the window above the sink. "If I don't do something drastic and soon, I'll carry you to my bed."

He heard her gasp and turned to face her, not bothering to hide the hunger that filled his body. "Remind me again why it's such a bad idea? Tell me why we're fighting something we both want. Because unless you can give me a solid reason in the next seven seconds, I'm taking you upstairs."

Susannah shivered. He was serious. And she didn't want to stop him. She wanted all the raw passion that exuded from every square inch of him. But they'd had reasons for not taking this extra step, reasons that had made good sense earlier.

"Because…" She paused and cleared her throat. "Because I'm only here temporarily. And things are complicated enough between us, and Flynn, already that we don't want to confuse them any more." He prowled forward and she stepped back, stopping when she hit the counter.

"I'll be leaving soon…" she finished uncertainly. It had sounded much more convincing the last time she'd said it—now it seemed flimsy.

"New plan." He leaned fists on the counter on either side of her, holding her in place. "You come to my bed now."

She opened her mouth to protest, but he laid a finger across her lips. "We go into this with no illusions, and no one will be hurt. We'll keep it separate from Flynn and he'll never know. You're leaving soon, so this will be short-term. We're both adults, we can deal with that. What we can't deal with is fighting this attraction," he said fiercely. "It's too damn strong. At least, it is for me."

"Doubly so for me," she said through a dry throat. Yet, a rebel part of her mind protested...she'd never slept with someone knowing it would go no further—purely for the physical pleasure. Could she do it? Indulge her desire for him and not let her heart get involved?

If the choice was between never experiencing Matthew's lovemaking or trying something new in having a short-term physical relationship, then the decision wasn't difficult at all.

"All right." She met his gaze. "Let's go with your new plan."

A shudder racked his large frame. "For days, I've barely been able to look at you without imagining touching your skin. I've wanted to kiss you right here—" his lips touched the place where the column of her throat met her shoulder "—so badly it's been keeping me awake at night."

The heat of his tongue on the vulnerable skin was intoxicating, drawing her under his dark spell. She brought her hands up to his shoulders so she didn't fall...and for the simple pleasure of touching him.

"What's been keeping you awake at night?" he murmured against her skin.

An image flashed into her mind—the bare skin she'd glimpsed on his neck when his top buttons had been undone that first morning. With fumbling fingers, she undid his shirt buttons to halfway down his torso and splayed her fingers on the warm skin she uncovered.

"This," she whispered, running her fingertips over the crisp hairs that were scattered across his chest, the heat inside her building.

He drew a sharp breath between his teeth. "Just that?"

"Starting with that."

In one smooth motion, he grabbed the back of his shirt, pulled it over his head and discarded it. The expanse of muscled chest that stood before her sent sharp anticipation zinging through her veins. His arms slid around her waist, and she leaned forward and pressed her lips to the skin just above a flat brown nipple.

"Susannah," he rasped then pulled her face up to kiss her hungrily. It was as darkly decadent as their first kiss, but this time it was so much more. There was no need to hold back; she could give free rein to all the passion she'd been holding in check, all the primal need that reared up inside her.

Although this kiss wasn't merely about giving—it was about taking what she wanted. And she wanted Matthew.

He wrenched his mouth away and began making a damp trail down past her chin. His cheek, covered in evening stubble, created a delicious abrasiveness as it brushed along her throat. She was caught in a whorl of desire—fire licking her veins, sensual fog filling her mind. Had she ever needed anyone, anything this desperately, this deeply?

Her fingers found the smooth planes of his back; felt the flex and release of his muscles as he moved. When his teeth gently sampled the skin of her collarbone, she dug her nails into the flesh near his spine.

"Tell me you want this as much as I do," he said, his tone half entreaty, half demand.

She put her hand over his heart and found the beat—it thundered like hers. Then she took his hand and placed it over her heart. "Both hearts racing. I want you, Matthew."

He replaced his hand with the velvet brush of his lips, then his teeth as he softly bit the flesh on the slope of her breast through the fabric, before his fingers tugged impatiently at the buttons on her top. Once he'd parted the sides of her blouse, his hot gaze lingered on her breasts, his fingers tracing over the white lace of her bra. Pressure coiled out from her belly to every square inch of her body. She moaned softly, and he squeezed his eyes shut.

"Too much," he said, his jaw tight. "It's too much."

With gentle roughness, he swept her up, onto the large wooden kitchen table, bunching her skirt to her hips, and she wrapped her legs around his waist. He swore when she pressed herself against the bulge in his trousers, but he didn't move away. His darkened gaze locked on hers with unwavering intensity and time stood still as, disconcertingly, her heart unfurled a fraction. She struggled against any scrap of emotional connection—this was purely physical. They'd agreed. Then he pressed himself closer and the moment was thankfully lost to the sensual thrall he so easily incited.

Needing to feel him properly, she reached for the button on his trousers and released it before pushing the zipper down and letting them drop to the floor. He hooked his thumbs in the waistband of his boxers and pushed them down the same path and finally she could hold his silken heat in her hands. He groaned and she allowed her fingers to explore the rigidness, to play, to tease.

A hand clamped around her wrist. "I'm too close—if you keep doing that, I'll embarrass myself."

He was close? His breathing was ragged, his pupils dilated. Yes, she'd known he wanted her, but seeing the extent of his desire gave her a jolt of feminine power.

His arms were around her, releasing her bra. She shrugged out of it and tossed it over a chair. He filled his palms with her breasts and she pushed closer, wanting even more contact. She wanted everything he had to give. He leaned down and took the peak of one breast in his mouth and she moaned his name.

As he transferred the attention to the other breast, his hands worked her panties down her legs and thrust them aside before coming back for her skirt. Not waiting for him to find the zipper at her side, she loosened it and lifted her hips so he could pull it out from under her.

Once it was gone, he smoothed a hand over the delta of her thighs then parted her with his fingers. Hypersensitive from wanting him for days on end, the touch jolted her and she bucked against him. He slid his fingers against her, and she became boneless from the intensity, from the pleasure.

But he didn't linger—he was back kissing her again, his arms holding her firmly against his body, and this time when she wrapped her legs around his waist, there were no barriers between them.

"Don't move," he rasped then pulled away and disappeared for endless moments. Her skin began to cool and she hoped to heaven that he'd gone for protection—any other reason would be too devastating to consider. When he reappeared seconds later, he was sheathed and ready, and she went a little dizzy with longing. She reached for him, found his arm and dragged him closer, but he needed no encouragement. His head came down and kissed her with breathless urgency, while his hands slid under her hips, tilting her toward him.

He broke the kiss, and between ragged breaths, said, "I can't wait."

"Then don't," she said. She'd already been waiting too long for him—it might only have been days in real time, but it had felt like an eternity.

He slid inside her and all the breath left her body. He was everywhere—filling her vision, filling her body, filling her mind... Finding and matching his gliding rhythm, she clung to him, climbing higher.

One of his hands left her hips and snaked behind her shoulders to bring her up to meet his mouth. Her insides wound tighter, too tight, but she couldn't slow the momentum while Matthew's relentless, exquisite pace reigned.

Impossibly soon, she was on the edge, wanting to wait, to

linger, to relish every second, while also wanting to soar higher, but he took the decision away with his uncompromising pace and she burst free, floating above the world, boundless. Even as she soared, she felt him follow and reach his own summit with a guttural cry.

All she could do for a long time was cling to him, stunned by the intensity of their lovemaking. Still held against his panting body, she wondered if his thoughts were the same, before he eased her back down onto the table.

"I'm sorry, Susannah," he said, his voice laced with self-recrimination.

She blinked, bringing his face and his words into focus. "Sorry for what?" Thinking back, she couldn't remember him hurting her or anything else to apologize for—just an explosive experience she didn't think would ever be matched.

He eased back and turned to rest a hip on the table beside her. "I wanted to make it perfect for you, but I just couldn't slow down."

She chuckled at the ridiculousness of saying sorry about something so glorious. "Didn't it look like I had a good time?"

"I have to admit, toward the end there, I barely noticed." He winced and she realized how serious he was. "I don't remember ever losing control like that before."

She took his lightly stubbled cheeks between her hands. "Let me assure you, Matthew, it was good for me. Excellent, in fact. No—" she grinned "—incredibly excellent." Despite the frantic rush—or perhaps because of it?—it had easily been the best of her life.

His shoulders relaxed and a slow-burn smile spread across his face. "Even so, I'd like to make it up to you."

Blissful contentment still permeated every cell of her body, and she raised a playful eyebrow. "You thinking of flowers?"

Without warning, he was on his feet, had hoisted her into the air and was cradling her close. "Nope."

"Sappy greeting card?" she asked, casually ignoring the sudden change of being held high in his arms.

As they made their way to the staircase, he snatched a kiss. "Not even close."

"So, tell me, Matthew—" she ran a fingernail across his chest "—how do you plan to make it up to me?"

"I'm going to do it again." He pressed a kiss to her cheek. "Slower." A lingering kiss on her lips. "Better."

Her skin quivered. "I'm not sure I can handle 'better,'" she said, and meant it. Anything more might make her lose consciousness altogether.

He arched an eyebrow and lifted her higher in his arms. "We're about to find out."

At the top of the stairs, her happy mood evaporated as he turned left instead of right—they were going to his room. He'd mentioned his room—his bed—earlier, but she hadn't put the pieces together until this moment.

His room in the marital house…the room he'd shared with Grace.

Nausea swelled up from her stomach. She scrambled out of his arms and planted her feet on the floor. "Matthew, I'm sorry, but I can't."

He frowned and glanced downstairs, toward the kitchen. "It's a bit late for qualms about making love with me—that horse has well and truly bolted."

The door down the hall taunted her, and she laid a hand over her belly to quell the sick feeling. "I can't go in there." Surely he could understand?

Still frowning, his gaze swung from her to the door down the hall and back again. "I don't see—" Then his eyes widened as understanding dawned. "Susannah, this wasn't Grace's room." He took her hand and led her to the first door, then opened it. It was decorated in deep blues, with a blue-gray quilt. A very masculine room—it reminded her more of the wine cellar than anything else in the house.

"I moved in here after she died. Her room is the next one down the hall—I've left it as it was for Flynn. He likes to go in and hold her things."

Cautiously she took a step farther into the room. An enlarged photo of waves crashing into rocks dominated one wall, cupboards and drawers made from cherry wood on the opposing wall. Dominating the room was a large cherrywood bed. The tension in her belly dissolved. This was Matthew's room, no doubt about it. And she liked it—it was a room to feel comfortable in, a room that felt like him.

He came to stand behind her and threaded his fingers through hers. She felt his naked body press against her back. "You're the first woman I've brought in here."

It had been a year since his wife had died. Before she could censor herself, she asked, "Not even—"

"No one," he said with finality as he nuzzled the sensitive spot behind her ear.

Despite knowing that shouldn't mean anything to her—there was nothing more than the physical between them—it did. She turned in his arms. "I shouldn't admit it—" to herself *or* to him "—but I like that."

"Glad to oblige." His hands slid from her waist up her rib cage. "Now, back to the conversation we were having earlier."

As her breath hitched, she wrapped her arms around his neck, allowing his hands free rein. "Which conversation was that?"

His fingers continued their languid journey, down her sides, over the curve of her hips, in crazy patterns across her back. "I have some making up to do."

"Ah, yes. And not with flowers or a greeting card." She leaned closer and took his earlobe into her mouth, satisfied when he drew in a sharp breath. Then she leaned back, and found his green gaze again darkened with desire. "So, how do you plan to do it?"

"I thought I'd start by—" he picked her up and laid her out on the bed "—and then perhaps add a bit of—" Holding her ankle, he bent one of her legs up and kissed the inside of her knee.

Everything inside her wound tight, and his tongue lazily traced upward, along the sensitive flesh of her inner thigh. When he reached the center of her, raw electricity burst through her body.

"You know," she said, breathing hard, "I'm not sure slower will actually be better this time."

He glanced up and grinned. "It's a shame you think that way. I plan to make this last all night."

She melted into the pillows behind her and gave herself up to the sinfully delicious prospect.

Six

Susannah stretched contentedly in Matthew's bed, feeling the heavenly slide of his naked skin against hers. Over the past four days, they'd fallen into a habit of taking the dessert she'd made to his room. Tonight it was a triple-chocolate mousse and, after an hour of eating it both from the glass and Matthew's body, Susannah lay sated.

"There's something I need to ask," he said, his voice rumbling in his chest under her ear. He moved one arm behind his head and, with the other around her waist, he pulled her closer against his side.

"Whatever it is, you've chosen a good time." She smiled, feeling much like a cat in the sun.

"I spoke to Flynn's doctor today, and he said Flynn's blood work had maintained the improvement. He can come home tomorrow."

Suddenly her whole body, the room, the world, felt lighter. She pulled back a few inches to see his face. "And you're only just mentioning this now? That's fabulous news!"

A smile tugged his mouth. "He's doing great, and as long as I take him for regular checkups, they're optimistic that he'll recover one hundred percent."

Then another implication of Flynn's improvement sank in and her stomach hollowed. She wouldn't be needed as a standby bone-marrow donor. Her reason for being in Charleston, in Matthew's house, no longer existed. She'd always known this was temporary, and Matthew had said they'd be going into their physical relationship with no illusions, but still, a crazy kind of panic bubbled up into her chest.

Despite being unable to meet his eyes, she was determined to handle the situation with poise and found an accepting smile. "I'll leave for Georgia in the morning, before he gets home."

"That brings me to my question." He lifted her chin with a knuckle and waited until she looked up into his endless green eyes. "I want someone stay with us for a week—just an extra pair of eyes to keep watch on him while he's in the early stages of recovery. I told him it would be my mother, but he asked if it could be you."

Stay? She blinked slowly, absorbing the concept. Spend more time with Matthew and his son? They hadn't wanted to make love in the first place because Flynn would sense something was different and get his hopes up. If she stayed longer, wouldn't that compound the sin?

Yet a rebel part of her heart—a maternal corner she'd tried to keep silent—wanted desperately to stay a little longer and get to know Flynn. And then there were the extra nights it would allow in Matthew's bed…

"You think this is a good idea?" she asked tentatively.

He released her chin and shoved a hand through his dark hair. "One of the nurses mentioned that Flynn might find it something of an anticlimax when he gets home, because he's had so many visitors and staff fussing over him. Home will seem quiet and uneventful in comparison. I have to admit, having someone like you, someone he likes and who would be a novelty would probably help keep his spirits up while he makes the transition. And the hospital tells me that keeping his spirits up is important to his recovery." There was vulnerability in his eyes, a need to provide this for his child when he'd been blocked from providing so much recently.

Matthew stroked a finger along her spine. "Will the extra leave be a problem?"

They were at the end of the second week of her leave already—she'd extended it with the option of another extension. Her boss had been understanding about the circumstances. In the three years she'd been at the bank, she'd rarely taken leave, so there would be enough to cover this, and her assistant could continue leading the team for another week. And they'd given Matthew's family a cover story for her stay that would work for another week—that he'd offered Grace's old friend a place to stay while Susannah applied for jobs in Charleston. He'd told them she wanted to move back from Georgia and Grace would have expected him to help. His family had seemed to accept the story.

But they weren't the major issues. She laid her head back on his chest. "What about Flynn becoming attached to me?"

"We make sure all the signals project that you're just a visitor, and we emphasize that you'll be going home in a week, so his expectations are managed."

Could it work? Could she spend extra time with that precious little boy without setting him up for hurt? Her mind raced with the possibilities.

"Do you really think we can do that?"

He pulled her closer, flush along his side. "I'm sure we can. Say yes."

"Yes." Without thought, the word slipped from her mouth but as soon as it was said, her heart lifted.

"Thank you." His eyes darkened. "And that's seven more nights of you in my bed—though we'll have to pretend you're sleeping in your room." One corner of his mouth kicked up. "Or we could do it the other way around. I might like the chance to sneak into your bedroom late at night."

The tantalizing thought sent a shiver flashing across her skin, and brought out her brazen side. "What would you be wearing?"

"A robe. In case I was caught," he drawled and arched a lazy eyebrow.

"Sensible." She traced a fingernail over his pectoral muscles and smiled when he shuddered. "And under that?"

"You'd find me as naked as I am now." His hand slid under the sheet, then feather-soft over her abdomen.

Her pulse quickened. "I'm rather partial to you being naked."

"Glad to hear it." His fingers walked a slow, sensual path up her ribs, toward her shoulders. "Because there's something I'd like to do when I reach your room and it works much better without my clothes."

"Would I be dressed?" she asked, allowing the sheet to be tugged away when his fingers reached it.

"No, you'd definitely be *un*—" he placed a kiss in the valley between her breasts "—dressed."

She reached down, found him ready and one by one wrapped her fingers around him. "As it turns out, we're both naked now."

He drew in a sharp breath and the muscles in his neck tightened. "I believe you're right."

"Why don't you give me a preview?" She wriggled, aligning their bodies the way she wanted them, and twined her arms behind his neck.

He positioned himself between her thighs then leaned down on forearms either side of her head to whisper in her ear. "Now?"

"Yeah, now," she said, wrapping her legs around his waist, urging him on.

"It would be something along these lines…"

Ignoring the doubts at the back of her mind, she let herself become lost in this man while she still had him.

* * *

As Matt held Susannah's door open in the hospital parking lot, he couldn't draw his eyes away from the long shapely leg that emerged. It peeped out from beneath the hem of her long skirt, heating his blood and scrambling his mind. The moment she was standing free, he curled one hand behind her back and one around her neck, then leaned her against the car.

A smile curved her mouth. "I hadn't realized parking lots had this effect on you."

"You have this effect on me," he growled a second before lowering his head and seeking her mouth. She parted her lips without hesitation and he sank into her sweet depths and the sheer oblivion kissing Susannah granted. Her hands crept up to lock behind him, pulling him impossibly closer.

"Any reason for that?" she asked breathlessly when he wrenched away. "Not that I'm complaining, mind you."

He smoothed the hair back from her face, memorizing everything about her expression in this moment—eyes dark and sleepy, lips rosy and damp, cheeks flushed. He had one more week of Susannah in his bed, and he planned to make the most of it. But for now, things would be more circumspect during daylight hours.

"Once we walk in those doors," he said, placing a final, chaste kiss on her Cupid's bow lips, "we'll be on our best behavior. No clues for Flynn to pick up."

"So this was like a last fling." Her hands released their grip behind his back and, with a light touch across his skin, found their way back to her sides.

"Until he goes to bed."

"I'm looking forward to it already," she whispered, her gaze focused on his mouth.

For a long moment he considered giving in to his body's demand for another kiss, but if he did, they might not leave this parking lot for hours. And he was anxious to get Flynn. He'd missed the little guy more than he could ever have predicted before he'd become a father.

He drew in a steadying breath and moved away from the temptation of Susannah. "Let's go."

They walked side by side, but his hands itched to touch her. To twine their fingers together, or to place a palm at the small of her back. He resisted—they couldn't send mixed signals to Flynn and let him think he might be getting a new mommy. The poor kid had enough to deal with right now without the inevitable letdown if that happened then realizing Susannah really was leaving. When Flynn was around, Susannah was a friend of the family, no more. He had to keep his hands to himself.

As they walked past the nurses' station, one of the nurses waved him over. "Good morning, Mr. and Mrs. Kincaid."

Beside him, Susannah stiffened, and he winced, well aware that they probably looked like a family unit. If anything, they'd look more like a family than when he and Grace had been with Flynn, considering the dimpled chin his boy shared with Susannah. Guilt reared up from the pit of his stomach and swamped him.

No matter how much he, Susannah and Flynn might *look* like a family, they weren't. Grace was the one who belonged here. He'd stolen this from her, and he had no right to bring another woman into the equation. It was unfair to Susannah, and a betrayal to Grace's memory.

"Just Mr. Kincaid," he said with a smile to soften the correction. "This is Ms. Parrish."

"Oh, I'm sorry, Mr. Kincaid, Ms. Parrish. I just wanted to tell you how thrilled we all are that Flynn's going home. He's become quite a favorite here."

"Thank you. I'm looking forward to getting him home." In fact, now he was inside the hospital, he was more than restless to get to his son, and his fingers began tapping away on his thigh.

The nurse glanced down at the chart on her desk. "You've spoken to the doctor already?"

"On the phone last night." The doctor had said he wouldn't be available this morning, but had passed on instructions for once Flynn was at home, and said he'd see them at their follow-up appointment.

"Excellent," the nurse said. "I've started his discharge paperwork. If you just drop in on your way out and sign the forms, we should be right to go."

They walked to the anteroom, not needing to stop and gown up this time. Since he was going home, Flynn was ready to interact with people who hadn't been through the decontamination procedures. The doctor had recommended limiting his contact to just family members for a while longer, and to tell anyone who was sick to stay away. None of which would be a problem—Matt would have moved mountains to make the environment safe for his son.

Flynn scampered to the end of his bed and threw his arms out as they entered his room, his cheeks pink with a healthy flush. "Daddeee!"

Matt picked him up, and held him tight. "Hey, kiddo."

Flynn returned the hug for about three seconds before he pulled away to announce, "Daddy, I can go home today."

"I'm counting on it," Matt said, grinning.

Then Flynn reached for Susannah. "Sudi! I can go home today."

She put her arms out and Matt passed his son to her, and watched them talk, heads together. Susannah's face had a beautiful softness, her affection for Flynn shining clearly.

Another wave of guilt engulfed him, making it difficult to breathe. This was Grace's role—she should be here, bringing her son home. She'd loved Flynn with everything inside her, occasionally to the exclusion of all else. And Flynn had loved her back with the same devotion. It was Matt's fault they'd been torn away from each other—in pressuring her to take a doomed flight he may as well have killed her with his own hands. He cursed himself to hell and back, as he'd often done since that awful day twelve months ago.

The door to the anteroom opened behind him and he turned to see Alan Sinclair's dark blond head pop around the door frame.

"Do you mind if I come in?" he asked, with an easygoing smile.

Momentarily surprised, Matthew hesitated before remembering a call his personal assistant had taken a few days ago from Sinclair. Matthew had given permission for Sinclair to visit, though he couldn't see why he'd want to. Nonetheless, he appreciated being asked. Basic respect. Jack Sinclair had simply assumed he'd be given access to Flynn, but Alan's courtesy confirmed the opinion Matt had been developing—Alan was twice the man Jack was.

He covered the ground to the entrance and offered his hand to Alan. "You just caught us. We're taking him home today."

"Glad I didn't come this afternoon." Alan glanced over at Flynn who was watching the exchange from Susannah's arms. "Who would I have given this teddy to if you'd already gone home?"

Flynn's face lit up when he saw the chocolate-brown bear with large blue eyes. Susannah had moved closer so Flynn was within reaching distance but still kept a protectively firm hold on him.

Having backup was as novel as it was nice, but Matt knew he couldn't allow himself to rely on it, so he reached for Flynn and held him on his hip.

"This is your—" grandfather's mistress's son "—Uncle Alan."

"Hello, Flynn," Alan said warmly, handing over the bear. "Do you like bears?"

"Yes." With wide eyes, Flynn surveyed the bear from all angles, obviously pleased with what he found by the grin that stretched his face. Matt put him down on the bed so Flynn could play with his new toy.

"And this is Susannah, a friend of ours." Matt turned to Susannah. "This is Alan Sinclair. You met his brother, Jack, a few days ago."

Alan offered his hand to Susannah. "Pleased to meet you, Susannah."

Matt watched Alan as Susannah took his hand. Did he notice the similarities between her and Flynn, putting two and two together the way the nurse had? Did others in his family suspect the truth about Flynn's parentage? He sighed and retrieved Flynn's empty bag from the cupboard. Maybe no one noticed how much Flynn resembled Susannah and he was getting paranoid.

Through the glass, a nurse held up some papers and Matt nodded. She'd obviously finished the discharge forms.

He turned back to Alan. "I hate to rush you, but we're just on our way home."

"Not a problem," Alan said with an easy smile. "I just wanted to drop this off. Nice to meet you, Flynn." He turned to Susannah. "And you, too, Susannah."

After Alan left, they packed Flynn's bags to the soundtrack of Flynn detailing which of his toys would be played with on his return to his own bedroom. Susannah glanced up and their eyes met in a moment of shared humor and optimism. It was balm to his soul to hear his son's enthusiasm—such a turnaround from the lethargic boy he'd brought into hospital not too long ago.

They were ready in minutes, and Matt carried Flynn's bags while Susannah pushed Flynn in a child's wheelchair the nurses provided, stopping to sign the forms on the way out. They left the wheelchair at the front door and Susannah lifted his son into her arms.

Seeing the nurse again brought her mistake about them being a couple to mind. Yet, watching Susannah and Flynn chatting away on the short walk to the car, he couldn't help observing how *right* the three of them looked together. How easily Susannah had slipped into their lives. Into Flynn's heart. Into Matthew's own bed.

Maybe this was all falling into place so easily because it was meant to be?

Could it be that easy—or was he fooling himself with a convenient half-truth?

They reached his car and, after stowing the bags in the trunk, Matthew took his son and strapped him into his seat before depositing a kiss on the top of his head. Then he turned to the woman who was causing his confusion.

"Thanks for coming," he said. As they passed behind the car where Flynn couldn't see, he slipped his hand around hers for an illicit two-second touch. "Flynn liked having you here."

"I was glad to do it," she said, but he saw the same confusion, the same doubts that were pursuing him, reflected in her eyes.

He opened her door and after she was in, he closed it and made his way around to the driver's side. As he slid into his seat, he turned to survey his passengers. "Ready to go?" he asked them.

"Yes," Flynn replied, beaming.

He met Susannah's eyes in a moment of pure understanding— the elation of bringing Flynn home, healthy and happy. The second time this morning she'd given him the simple pleasure of sharing a parenting moment. He'd missed that beyond measure. Yet it was shadowed by the knowledge that they were playing with explosives, perhaps letting themselves be lured in too deep.

He turned the key, ready to drive this imitation family home.

Seven

Two hours later, Susannah was sitting with Matthew and Flynn around a garden setting in the glass conservatory eating banana and chocolate-chip muffins. Before sunrise, she'd been up baking an assortment of food she hoped might tempt a three-year-old. So far, given Flynn's enthusiastic reaction to the brunch picnic, it seemed she'd succeeded. Matthew had eaten more than she'd expected, and the fact that father and son were happily devouring her food made a contended joy rise higher than it should.

The phone rang, and Matthew reached for the cordless he'd brought with him and handed it to Flynn. "That will be Grandma."

Flynn's face beamed and he eagerly took the handset. "Grandma?" he asked into the receiver. The reply must have been affirmative, because then he was off, a stream of chatting, telling all his news about his hospital stay.

Matthew leaned over, his warm breath brushing the shell of

her ear as he spoke. "Grace's parents. They ring every Sunday at ten o'clock."

Even with her body's predictable response to his nearness, something she couldn't define twisted painfully in her belly. "That's great they take an interest in him."

"They adore him," he said, watching his son. "Grace was an only child, so now she's gone, Flynn is the only grandchild they'll ever have. They come and stay often, and never miss a Sunday call."

He didn't have to say the rest. It hung in the air between them—Grace's parents were another reason he could never disclose that Susannah was Flynn's biological mother. If he was the only grandchild they would ever have, then how could he tell them they had no genetic connection to the little boy? Rob them of their remaining link to the daughter they'd tragically lost? And she wouldn't want him to—it would be too cruel.

"Daddy," Flynn said, his face serious, obviously with an important mission.

Matthew turned to him, a gentle smile on his face. "Yes?"

"Grandma wants to talk wif you." He passed the phone to his father then turned to Susannah. "Can I have ano'ver muffin, please?"

"Sure, sweetie," she said.

She handed him one, and while he ate, she watched Matthew talking to his mother-in-law, her heart unexpectedly sinking. They were obviously on familiar and friendly terms—laughing and chatting casually. The scene zoomed out in her mind, leaving her dizzy then came into clear focus.

This was Grace's family. Grace's parents on the phone, who'd rung Grace's little boy. They were in Grace's house, and she was sleeping with Grace's husband.

Her vision swam and she dug her nails into her palms.

This wasn't her life—she'd simply slotted into a Grace-shaped hole in Flynn and Matthew's life.

At least there was a time limit—in a week she'd be back in

her own life in Georgia and Grace's family would go back to functioning without her. The thought wasn't as comforting as she'd hoped.

The next morning at breakfast, Matt was on top of the world. His son was home and on the mend, and he'd spent half the night making sweet, glorious love to Susannah. Things were looking up.

"Does anyone want more pancakes?" Susannah asked, glancing over to where he and Flynn sat at the kitchen table.

"Me!" Flynn called gleefully.

Matt took their plates to the stove where Susannah was making another batch of her blueberry-and-oat pancakes, pausing to admire how good she looked in his kitchen. He couldn't be here with her and not think of making love to her, her sumptuous curves draped over the table, clinging to him as she found release. His body heated now, not nearly sated enough even after the night they'd shared.

Drawing her into his arms wasn't an option when Flynn was in the room, but he'd be sure to make up for it the moment they had some privacy. Make up for it and then some.

"Here you go." Susannah flipped two pancakes onto each plate. Her cheeks were faintly flushed from the heat of the stove and all he could think about was how they took on the same flush when he was inside her.

He cleared his throat and hauled himself back into the present. "Have I mentioned these are the best pancakes I've tasted?" He put Flynn's plate in front of him and poured some more maple syrup over the golden creations.

"You might have," she said, winking at Flynn, "but I don't mind hearing it again."

The doorbell went, and Matt threw her a grin before heading out to answer it. When he pulled the front door open, his mother stood there and, without bothering with a greeting, he pulled her into a bear hug. She'd been great while Flynn was in the hospital—no, since Grace had passed—so it was good she was here now for Flynn's first breakfast at home.

When he let her go, she smoothed down his hair. "How's Flynn this morning?"

"Better," he said, closing the door behind her. "And eating like a trouper."

"Your omelets?" she asked with a dubious expression.

"Hey, he likes my omelets." He frowned in mock annoyance. "But, no, Susannah's still here. She made pancakes."

Her eyes were instantly alert. "That friend of Grace's?"

"That's the one." Before she could ask more questions, he ushered her through to the kitchen.

"Nanna!" Flynn called when he saw her. "Sudi made pancakes wif oats in them!"

"Did she?" His mother looked curiously at Susannah and back to her grandson then him. "That sounds marvelous." She walked over and deposited a kiss on Flynn's sticky cheek.

"You've already met Susannah?" he asked, wary of what was going on in his mother's mind. Perhaps it had been too much to hope that his family wouldn't question the story he'd fed them about Susannah's presence. At the time, helping out an old friend of Grace's while she looked for work back in Charleston had seemed a good enough reason to explain her stay. He hadn't worried too much about their reaction, which, in retrospect, could have been a mistake.

"Yes," his mother answered. "We met in the hospital."

Susannah turned and smiled brightly. "It's lovely to see you again, Mrs. Kincaid. Have you eaten breakfast, or can I offer you a pancake?"

Her smile hit him squarely in the chest, so to cover he headed for the coffeemaker. "And I was just about to make coffee."

He reached around Susannah for the jar of coffee grounds then glanced up at his mother for her answer, and found her watching him with that curious expression on her face again.

She started, as if realizing she'd been staring then smiled. "I'd love a coffee. And if you have a few minutes, Matthew, there's something I'd like to discuss."

Susannah moved around him with synchronicity as she put the empty pan in the sink and he continued with the coffee. "Flynn and I'll be okay on our own if you want some privacy."

"Thank you, dear," his mother said with a strange touch of self-satisfaction. "That's very thoughtful."

He finished the coffee, left one mug for Susannah, then took the other two and followed his mother into the parlor. She had far too much swing in her step for his peace of mind. She was planning something. They sank into facing couches and he handed her a cappuccino.

"You and Susannah," she began.

He rolled his shoulders back, ready to nip whatever she was thinking in the bud. "Are just friends."

She took a slow sip of her drink, watching him over the brim. "Somehow I expected you'd say that, yet why don't I believe you?"

"She was a—"

"Friend of Grace's. I've heard the story," she said with a dismissive wave of her hand. "But there's something more between you."

He opened his mouth to deny it, then changed tack and decided to pump her for information instead of the other way around. Casually he leaned back and rested an arm along the back of his couch. "Why do you say that?"

"A mother knows," she said, her tone flippant.

He leveled a sardonic stare at her and held it. It was a ploy that usually worked on her and he wasn't disappointed this time, either.

She shrugged and tried to hide her grin. "How about we say that when you look at each other, the sparks that fly are strong enough to light the whole of Charleston." Her expression sobered into an expression of pure parental reprimand. "However,

I won't lie and say I'm happy that she's here under your roof. How about she comes to stay with me and—"

"Not going to happen," Matthew said, cutting that idea off before it was fully voiced. Susannah was staying right here with him for however many days she had left in Charleston. "Do you think anyone else has noticed?"

"I doubt it," she said soothingly and took another sip of her cappuccino. "You're my son, and I can't help but keep an eye on you."

Visions rose of his entire family knowing and taking every opportunity to tease him then rumors leaking back to Flynn. He needed to end this now. "She's leaving soon, so we'd rather this didn't become public knowledge."

"Don't let her go."

The words had been so simply, so starkly delivered that he did a double take. "Pardon?"

"There's been something different about you lately. You've been worried sick about Flynn, I've seen that, but there has also been a…glow from the inside. It's like you're waking up from a deep sleep."

Matt groaned. His mother was well on her way to creating an epic romance for him with Susannah. He rubbed a finger across his forehead. "Don't get your hopes up."

"Darling," she said, her tone suddenly more serious, "we have something awful in common. We've both lost a spouse to death." She paused and he recognized the confused flash of conflicting emotions that played across her face from when he'd felt the same. "It's not something I'd ever wish for one of my children, and I would have done anything to spare you the last twelve months."

He put his coffee down on a side table and leaned forward to capture her hands between his. "I know you would. And I love you for that."

"Then promise me one thing."

"Okay," he said warily.

"If you're in love with her, don't hide it." Her voice faltered, but she regrouped then her chin kicked up. "Just promise me you won't hide it."

There was more to what she was saying. He frowned, trying to read her expression. Perhaps she was thinking about his father's hidden affection for Angela Sinclair?

"I'm not in love with her, and that won't change." He'd given his heart away once and it was decimated when things fell apart with Grace. He'd never offer it again. Whatever was—temporarily—going on between him and Susannah, it did not, would not, involve his heart.

"If you say so." There was a resigned affection in her voice that he remembered her using when he was a boy and she hadn't believed him.

He released her hands and picked up his mug of coffee again. "What did you want to talk to me about?"

She reached into her handbag and withdrew two tickets. "You've been courting Arnold Larrimore from Larrimore Industries as new business for TKG, haven't you?"

"I have." Getting his business would go a long way to plugging the hole that was created when people jumped ship after the scandal about his father had hit the papers.

"I happen to know he'll be at the Barclays' fundraiser on Sunday." She waggled the tickets in her hand triumphantly. "I managed to get us invited."

His mother's social connections through her charity work had been of great value to Matt's role as Director of New Business for TKG. She procured introductions, tickets to events, dinner party invitations and general access to a social scene the family didn't normally mix in. And since Grace died, his mother had accompanied him to any of the events where he needed a plus one.

"Great scouting." He'd do most anything to be able to announce to the board that he'd snared Arnold Larrimore's account and put TKG back on more solid footing.

"There's only one problem," she said, handing him the tickets.

He took them, with a sinking sensation in his stomach—he had a feeling where this was going. "Which is?"

"I don't think I can make it." Her face fell—a picture of tragic disappointment. "I've turned my ankle, and couldn't possibly spend an entire night in heels."

He glanced down at her perfectly normal ankle and back up again. "It seemed fine when you walked in here."

"It's been a strange injury." Her eyelids fluttered in feigned distress. "It comes and goes. In fact, I can feel it starting to ache now."

He narrowed his eyes. His mother was a good liar, but this had to be the lamest story she'd ever concocted. Obviously she'd created it on the spot. "Perhaps you should stay here for the day with it elevated. I'll put ice on it now then wrap it later."

"I think I'd be better heading for home. Pamela will know what to do. But you really should go to the Barclays' fundraiser." She pretended to think. "I know, take Susannah! I can stay with Flynn—a little turned ankle will be fine here with him."

"Mother," he growled, "you're trying to set me up."

She stood, and picked up her handbag. "I have no idea what you're talking about. Must dash," she said, leaning to kiss his cheek.

She took three steps before she remembered to limp. Matt shook his head and showed her out.

Later that night, Susannah opened her bedroom door to a light knock, to find Matt lounging in the doorway, one arm behind his back and a sexy grin on his face. His closely cropped hair was damp. Seemed he'd showered then pulled on a polo shirt and loose trousers afterward. Her entire body tingled with anticipation. How would she ever leave this man when the time came?

"Evening," he said, then drew her against him with one arm, capturing her mouth with the ease of a predator assured of his prey. She fell into the kiss with no regard for anything but tasting his essence, of dissolving into him. His lips were so warm, exerting just the right pressure. She gripped the front of his shirt as her knees wobbled. Reality ceased to exist—she was in a blissful place outside time and space that she only found with Matthew.

After an eternity, he slowly drew back, chest heaving, pupils large in his luminescent green eyes. He held up a bottle of wine and two sparkling glasses. "Fancy a nightcap?"

Still gripping his shirt, she attempted to reorient herself to her surroundings. To breathing. She released him then opened the door wider to let him through. "Let's start with that."

He poured a glass each then sprawled on her bed. Propped on one elbow, he looked far too comfortable and desirable. She took a memory picture to keep with her after she left Charleston that could sustain her in what she suspected would be long, lonely nights without him.

"My mother guessed there's something between us," he said with a rueful smile.

Her hand flew to her mouth. She'd thought they'd been careful. "Oh, I'm sorry, Matthew."

"She won't tell anyone." He held out a hand and when she took it, he dragged her down to sit on the bed with him. "And she still thinks you're just one of Grace's friends."

Grace. Her stomach lurched. In this family, with this man, everything always came back to Grace. It always would, which—she straightened her back—was just how it should be. Her sensitivity to being sidelined shouldn't affect how Matthew and his family operated. She was temporary—soon, she'd be returning to the life waiting for her in Georgia, her mother, her friends and a senior position at the bank.

"She left two tickets for a fundraiser on Sunday," Matthew said, pulling one of her feet onto his lap. "I need to go for work—I'm targeting a new account. Do you want to come?"

The magic his fingers were producing on the soles of her feet momentarily distracted her, which was dangerous. If she wasn't on her guard, she might actually agree to go.

"Where is it?" she asked, stalling for time.

He reached for her other foot and began to give it the same attention as the first. "At the Barclays' mansion on one of the islands of the Outer Banks."

She wrapped one arm around herself and sipped her wine. When she'd been a teenager, her grandparents had often taken her to society parties and elite fundraising events, and she'd hated each and every one of them. The feeling of not quite belonging, of being an impostor wearing a pretty dress and pretending to be as cultured and sophisticated as the other guests. She wouldn't return to that world. It was soul-destroying.

She shrugged apologetically and shook her head. "I'm sorry, I haven't brought anything with me I could possibly wear to an event like that."

"Not a problem," he said without missing a beat. "I'll buy you something."

Her skin cooled. Pulling her feet from his lap, she turned to face him. "You can't buy me a dress, Matthew." It would be far too…bizarre. Inappropriate. If he bought her things while she was having a physical relationship with him, she'd start to feel like a kept woman. Matthew's father had kept a woman on the side, as had many of her grandfather's friends. People from that world—Matthew's world—thought differently about people and relationships.

"I need someone to go with me," Matthew said. "These things are always attended in couples. If you'll come, I'll cover your expenses."

Put like that, it sounded reasonable. Yet there was resistance to the idea deep in her chest. Having a temporary physical relationship with Matthew while staying in Charleston was one thing, but becoming entangled in his world of wealth and privilege…it scared her.

She tucked her legs beneath her and tried again. "I'm already living in your house, eating—"

"Susannah," he said, cutting her off, "you came to Charleston to do Flynn and me a favor. You've stayed on because we asked you to, again as a favor. And now *I'm asking if you'll help me out by attending a fundraising event as my guest*. You've done nothing but give since you got here. At the very least, let me buy you a dress to wear while you're doing one of those favors."

Oh, sweet Lord, he knew how to get what he wanted. *I'm asking if you'll help me out by attending a fundraising event as my guest*. How could she say no to such a small favor?

She let out a long breath. "It doesn't feel right." Attending the event or letting him buy the dress.

"But you'll do it." His confident, devastating smile spread across his face and she was lost.

"Okay," she said, and hoped she wouldn't regret this.

Eight

Matt stepped into the exclusive boutique, his hand at Susannah's waist ensuring she entered with him, even if it was reluctantly. Flynn was spending the day with his grandmother and Pamela so Matt could have a full day at TKG, and he'd slipped out to meet Susannah here during his lunch hour.

He was determined she would have something perfect, that she liked, and he had a feeling that if he left her alone, she'd prioritize economy over those factors. He'd never met a woman so determined not to be given anything.

His personal assistant was in her sixties and always wore the same severe outfits, so he'd gone to RJ's assistant this morning for advice on the best store to take Susannah. Brooke had been excellent, giving him choices and not once asking the obvious question of why he'd want the name of a women's clothing store—the precise reason he hadn't asked any of his sisters. He knew Brooke could be discreet.

The saleswoman glided over and gave them a welcoming smile. "How may I help?"

He moved Susannah infinitesimally forward with a hand at her back. "We'd like a cocktail gown. It's for an elite gathering, so quality is paramount."

He felt Susannah's invisible flinch at his not so subtle message about money being no object, but he was unrepentant. She deserved the best the store had to offer.

"Of course, sir," the saleswoman said. "If ma'am would follow me?"

As the other woman moved away, Susannah leaned over and whispered, "I still don't like this. I can buy my own dress."

"We've discussed this. I'll be happier if I buy it."

She shot him a resigned look before following the sales assistant deeper into the store.

In fact, there was something immensely satisfying in being able to give her this. Perhaps it was in his DNA—providing for his lover. Perhaps it was marking her as his own with expensive fabrics. Or perhaps it was as simple as wanting to give something back after all she'd given him and his son, to bring her joy.

The saleswoman reappeared and showed Matt to an upholstered chair with a good view of the curtain screening the generously sized change room where Susannah had apparently gone.

Within minutes, she tentatively stepped out, wearing a figure-hugging royal-blue dress that flared from her knees. His brain froze, and all he could do was stare—and hope he wasn't making a fool of himself. The color made her blue eyes bluer, highlighted her porcelain skin and the shape drew attention to each curve, making him wish they were home and he could explore them himself.

"I usually choose much simpler designs," she said. "But the saleswoman was fairly insistent about this one."

He cleared his throat before he could speak. "It's stunning."

She gave him an appreciative smile then slipped behind the curtain again. While she was gone, he tried to regulate his breathing. Who knew shopping for women's clothes would be this dangerous to his health?

A few minutes later she emerged in an oriental red sheath with a mandarin collar. Cut into the fabric was a large teardrop shape that exposed the top of her cleavage. He restrained a groan.

"Not that one," he rasped. There was no way he wanted other men seeing her in that dress. They'd be imagining her out of it. The way he was right now.

"Yes, I don't think red is my color," she said, surveying it in the mirror.

"Sweetheart, if red was any more your color, I'd have to pick myself up off the floor. I only meant it might be too sexy for the Barclays' fundraiser."

She looked down at the hole over most of her décolletage and grinned. "You're probably right."

She disappeared and returned in a floating dress that had an overlay of sheer blush pink fabric. The bodice was fitted, then it fell in soft drapes to below her knees. It was pure Susannah. Fresh and free and feminine. Sweet, yet sexy as all hell.

She turned in front of the mirror, looking at it from all angles and he watched her, heart thundering as if it would explode. If he'd wanted her before, seeing her in a different environment, in these clothes, the need was more than anything he'd ever experienced.

Her gaze flicked to his in the mirror, and he could see she was surprised by the dress, liked it.

"That's the one," he said.

She arched an eyebrow. "Do I get some say?"

"Of course," he said, knowing he was calling her bluff. "Do you like it?"

"Why, yes, I do," she said with an overly innocent smile. "Thank you for asking."

She twisted to find the price tag, but he leaped to his feet and clasped her hand before she could read it. "Don't look. Just let me buy it for you."

Their gazes held and he could feel the battle she waged inside herself. It had been momentous for her to accept him buying the dress in the first place, he knew that. She was obviously more used to giving than receiving. But to not even know the amount she'd be indebted to him for would take a leap of faith.

Finally she nodded, and he felt a surge of masculine satisfaction.

Once they'd told the saleswoman of their decision and he'd paid, they were back out on the pavement, the dress wrapped in tissue paper and in a bag that was looped around his fingers.

"Is there anything else you need?" He knew accessories were important, but wasn't sure on the details. Matching shoes, perhaps?

"A gelato," she said with certainty.

As the words registered, he did a double take. This woman never stopped surprising him. He tried—but failed—to keep a grin from emerging. "You need a gelato?"

"There's a store on the next block that sells the best in the state." Her face lit with enthusiasm, which was undeniably infectious. "Let me buy you one."

He couldn't remember the last time he'd gone out for gelato. It seemed too whimsical a thing to do. There was a container of strawberry ice cream in the freezer at home for Flynn, but it wasn't something he would take a serving of for himself.

However, he recognized the nature of her offer—accepting his purchase of the dress had been uncomfortable, and she was trying to reestablish the balance by giving him something back. It might be only a small gift in return, but the spirit of the exchange would allow her to retain some dignity.

He took her hand and interlaced their fingers. "A gelato would be good."

She smiled broadly and led the way. As they walked down the street, hand in hand, an odd feeling crept over him—the people passing by would think he and Susannah were a couple. In a proper relationship. And, stranger still, he didn't mind the feeling. He hadn't been on the lookout for someone new in his life, but he rather liked the feeling of having a gorgeous woman by his side.

Susannah herself was only here temporarily, and besides, he had a feeling that when she entered a long-term relationship, she'd want it all—love and marriage. Neither of which he would ever offer a woman again. Been there, done that, paid the price. Dealing with falling out of love with his wife, the mother of his child, had been the hardest thing he'd ever done. The pain as he and Grace had sorted through the wreckage of their marriage wasn't something he'd ever let be repeated.

But maybe at some point in the future, he should consider a longer term relationship. Obviously he'd keep it separate from Flynn—the last thing that kid needed was a procession of Matt's girlfriends to attach to then lose. Yet he couldn't help but remember Susannah's comment over breakfast her first morning in his house.

You can't live just for your work and Flynn. You have needs, too, Matthew.

Maybe after things settled down with The Kincaid Group and Flynn was one hundred percent better, he'd think about finding someone amenable to a quiet, part-time relationship.

"There it is," Susannah said, pointing to a storefront with a bright yellow-and-white striped awning. "Have you been here before?"

"Can't remember it." He looked at the people casually ordering inside. "Then again, I'm not sure I've lined up for ice cream since I was a kid." Until Susannah had converted him to desserts, he'd been more of a cheese-platter guy. Now he was about to eat a serving of sugar in the middle of the day.

A young man with a white paper hat sauntered down to their end of the counter. "What can I get you folks?"

"We'll need to try a couple of samples first," Susannah said. "It's my friend's first time."

"No problem." He reached for a cup of small plastic spoons. "Which ones?"

Susannah turned and looked up at him expectantly. Matt dug his hands into his pockets and surveyed the variety of flavors—everything from tiramisu to mango. While he read the labels, he indicated that Susannah should go ahead and order, so she asked for a double serving of pink grapefruit, no cone.

"I'll try the grapefruit," Matt said to the young guy, who then scooped a small spoon into the pale pink ice confection and handed it over the counter.

It touched his taste buds with an explosion of flavor—sharp tang and sweet simultaneously. The effect woke up every cell in his body. "I'll have that one," he said.

Susannah laid a delicate hand on his forearm. "You can't have the first one you taste, Matthew. Try another couple first."

He'd always adhered to the principle that you took what you wanted, but this was Susannah's excursion so he deferred to her plan. "The passion fruit and the amaretto."

The guy behind the counter handed him two more spoons. Both were good, but neither had the startling effect of the first one.

"A double serving of the grapefruit in a cup," he said.

They took their gelato and Matt looked around at the tables. "Inside or outside?" he asked.

"Outside," she said without hesitation. "It's gloriously warm for February and I don't want to waste it."

He held the door open for her, remembering the day she'd wanted to eat breakfast in the courtyard. And how she'd looked like a goddess with her face turned to the early morning sun. He'd been spellbound.

"You really like being outside, don't you?"

They found an empty picnic-style table on the paved area to the side of the store and sat down. A spoon loaded with pink gelato disappeared into her mouth, and then emerged empty from between closed lips. He waited while she swallowed, feeling his blood begin to heat.

A dreamy expression filled her eyes. "Sunshine and breeze, Matthew. You can't beat them."

"You know," he said without thinking, "that's a good way to describe you."

She paused with the spoon halfway to her mouth and an adorable line appeared between her brows. "What is?"

"You've swept into my life like a fresh breeze. And wherever you are, it's like there's sunshine." As soon as the words were out of his mouth, he felt stupid and wanted to snatch them back. Spouting bad lines of pseudopoetry? RJ would laugh his head off.

But Susannah simply smiled. "Thank you, that's a lovely thing to say."

She took another spoonful of gelato and he followed suit, watching her as he ate. There was something about Susannah that sparkled from within, made him want to understand as much as he could about what made her tick.

"Will you tell me something personal if I ask?"

"Depends." She smiled, tucking a pale silken strand of hair behind her ears. "Why not try me?"

"Was it as easy to give up Flynn in reality as you've said?" Since Flynn's health scare, when a little devil had been on Matt's shoulder, taunting him with the possibility of losing his son, he'd wondered about Susannah's act of giving Flynn to him in the first place. "I just can't imagine handing him to someone."

Absently she stirred the gelato in her cup. "It was nothing like what you'd go through now if you lost him," she said quietly, bringing her gaze back to him. "I knew from the start what I was doing. In my mind, I always thought of him as your baby. Yours and Grace's."

He sat back in his seat as she ate more of her gelato. That sounded reasonable in theory, but putting it into practice was surely a different story. "You never thought about changing your mind?"

"If you and Grace had changed your minds—" she paused,

as if choosing her words carefully "—and said I could have kept him, I would have been over the moon. But he was your baby from the start, so I didn't dream of a future with him."

"You're amazing," he said and meant it. Susannah Parrish possessed the most unselfish heart he'd come across.

She stared down at her paper cup for long moments and when she looked up at him again, her eyes glistened. "When I was sixteen, I lost a baby."

All the air left his lungs as the weight of her loss hit him squarely in the chest. He reached across the table and grasped her hand. "I'm sorry."

She squeezed his fingers. "It was an accidental pregnancy, but as soon as I knew, I loved that baby with everything inside me."

Susannah pushed her cup to the side of the metal picnic table. She hadn't spoken about that dear baby since he'd died. The whole period in her life wasn't something she let herself dwell on. Usually. But Matthew was so easy to talk to, and he needed to hear this, to understand.

"I got pregnant because I was angry at my grandparents."

His head tilted to the side. "Their tug-of-war for you?"

"Yes, but it was more than that. Looking back, I was such a good kid. But it was never enough for them. There were constant lectures about being 'a lady,' and expectations I would perform better next time and be the proper social accessory. I was easy prey for a teenage boy." Her hands circled her throat. "I met him at one of my grandparents' parties and in my one act of teenage rebellion I went with him out to the secluded gardens and, inevitably, became pregnant."

With understanding in his eyes, he shook his head. "It might have been only one rebellion, but it was a doozy."

"We told our parents and though no one was thrilled, his parents were downright manipulative. They demanded I sign a contract to place the baby for adoption as soon as it was born so nothing would interfere with the glorious future they had planned for their son."

She clearly remembered the feeling of being overwhelmed by a rich family who stuck together. One who thought they could get whatever they wanted by pushing hard enough. Matthew's family seemed nice, but her experience of families with inherited wealth had been frightening—they thought and operated differently than other people. Flynn would experience that as an insider—the Kincaids would stick by him through thick and thin—but she would never get involved with a family like that. It had been the reason she'd been reluctant at first to get involved with Grace's surrogacy proposal. But seeing the strength of Grace's need, and her own mother's financial desperation, had convinced her it was the right thing to do. Still, she'd taken the contract Grace had given her to a lawyer before signing it to make sure she was fully protected in case things went pear-shaped.

To the wealthy, outsiders were always expendable to some degree. Just like her mother had been with her father's family.

She glanced at Matthew and saw the disapproval of how she'd been treated in his narrowed eyes. Despite being part of one of those families, he was a good man, but the powerful bonds with his family were evident in everything he did. As was how accustomed he was to getting what he wanted through money and influence.

"That was unforgivable of them," he said.

Tears pricked at the back of her eyes, both from what had happened back then, and for Matthew's support now. "My mother thought so, as well. She wasn't happy that I was pregnant so young, but she was thrilled about having a grandchild. I refused to sign that contact. I was keeping him, no matter what."

"What happened?" he asked, voice deep with concern.

"He was born too early. They said that sometimes happens when the mother is so young—there was no other explanation, no other reason. Good news for being able to carry Flynn years later, but it didn't help when I was a teenager and wanted answers." Her eyes drifted closed, as if to protect her against the pain. Yet that merely provided a blank slate for the memories. "The doctors worked hard to help him, and he made it to three weeks old, but his little lungs and organs simply weren't developed enough to handle this life. We never even brought him home from the hospital."

"Oh, Susannah, I'm sorry." He stood and pulled her out of her seat and into his arms. "What was his name?"

"William," she said against his chest. "After my dad."

He stroked a hand over her hair. "A good name."

Despite wanting to stay in his arms and soak up the support he offered, she pulled back and drew him down to the seat beside her. It was important he hear this.

"Matthew, I told you this story to show you the difference. I was a mess of grief when I lost William. And I still think about how my life would be if he'd lived. But Flynn was always meant to be yours. I won't deny that it was a wrench to give him up, but nothing like losing William."

He nodded and cupped her cheek. "Because you'd let yourself love William."

"Yes," she whispered. "I reminded myself all the time that Flynn belonged to you."

A ball of emotion lodged in his throat. "I don't know if I've ever said thank you for him. I know we said some things at the hospital about how grateful we were, but I never sat down like this, looked you in the eye and said it." He reached for her hands and clasped them tightly between his. "Thank you, Susannah Parrish. You did a beautiful thing in giving us our baby."

The sincerity in his bottomless green eyes touched a secret place inside her. "One thing I learned from losing William is that you can't put a price on the gift of life. It's infinitely precious. And I was glad, deep in my soul, to be able to give you and Grace that gift."

"I believe that of you." He leaned forward and placed a kiss on the top of her head. "What about the future? You've had two babies, but you didn't get to keep either of them. Will you have another?"

"I'd love to raise a baby. Or two or three." A vision rose of a little girl who matched Flynn, with Matthew's coloring and a dimple in her chin. She wore a purple cotton dress with a big bow at the front and held out her chubby arms. The picture was so clear she ached to draw the girl close. Matthew's voice dragged her from the dreamlike trance.

"You'll be a fabulous mother."

Horrified by the direction of her thoughts, she looked away. This was a temporary situation. She was going back to Georgia in a few days. If she let herself become enamored by fantasies, she'd wind up making bad decisions.

"Did you see they sell the gelato by tub, as well?" she said brightly, changing the direction of the conversation without any subtlety. "We could take some home to Flynn. What's his favorite?"

"Strawberry." Matthew rose from his seat, either not noticing or choosing not to comment on the abrupt change of subject. "But I'll get a tub of pink grapefruit as well for us." He dropped his voice. "I think it will taste even better tonight in bed."

Nine

Walking through the entranceway of the Barclays' mansion on Matthew's tuxedo-clad arm transported Susannah back ten years. The scene was awash with soft light and everything sparkled as these events always did, from the cocktail dresses of the female guests, to the gleaming marble and cut-glass chandeliers.

She'd attended similar events as a teenager with her grandparents, where they'd dress her up and parade her around. Their son—her father—was gone, and their two daughters had moved interstate, so her grandparents had relished the chance for a substitute child to use as a social accessory. The trip on the way had been full of instructions.

Don't scratch your nose.

Don't touch your hair and ruin the hairdresser's work.

Do smile (but only in the aloof, sophisticated style they'd made her practice).

Do seem interested in everything people tell you, but never laugh too hard or shriek. Not that she remembered shrieking; she'd been a quiet girl, but her grandparents left nothing to chance. She was there representing them, and her behavior was of vital importance.

Going home to her mother again where she could be herself had always been a relief. She could even scratch her nose if she felt the need.

She'd sometimes wondered whether her grandparents knew anything about her at all, or only saw a dress-up doll they could mold and shape to the image they wanted.

A shiver passed across her skin as she thought about meeting them here tonight, but they had a holiday place in Florida they used in January and February. And their friends hadn't seen her since she was a teenager, so hopefully none would recognize her as an adult.

"Are you okay?" Matthew asked close to her ear. "You seem a little strained."

She smiled up at him. "I'm good." Tonight was important to him; he needed her to help. As fate would have it, she was here again, being someone else's accessory, but this time she'd chosen the role. She could use all the skills her grandparents had taught her, ones that had then been refined during her work in public relations, for Matthew's benefit.

"What's your plan?" she asked him.

He cast a glance around the room, looking as reluctant to be here as she was. "Find my target, sell him on TKG and get out."

She chuckled. "How about a more subtle approach?"

"What do you suggest?" he asked, grabbing two glasses of champagne from a passing waiter.

"We mingle, work the room a bit, perhaps laying ground-work for future new business, then when an opportunity that feels natural arises with the client you're targeting, you chat with him and build a relationship."

"So less brash than my usual method?" His eyebrow arched at an amused angle.

"With many businesspeople, your forthright approach would

be pitch-perfect. But the people here will respond better to good manners and subtlety."

"Good point." His arm moved out from under her hand and slid around her waist. "Okay, let's do it."

An older woman with a heavy necklace Susannah knew was made of real diamonds and sapphires finished talking to the people who'd arrived before them and made her way over.

"Good evening, I'm Lydia Barclay, your hostess."

"Nice to meet you, ma'am," Matthew said. "I'm Matthew Kincaid, and this is Susannah Parrish."

"Kincaid?" Her eyes narrowed as her gaze raked him up and down. "You must be Elizabeth's son. We're on the board of the Arts Trust together."

"She speaks highly of you," Matthew said smoothly and flashed his devastating smile.

Mrs. Barclay fluttered her eyelashes, apparently charmed. "Let me introduce you to my dear friends, Mr. and Mrs. Raleigh."

Over the next twenty minutes, they slowly mingled with other guests and Susannah relaxed into her role. She remembered an occasional person from parties she'd been to years ago, but she was relieved that no one recognized her as an adult, avoiding any messy questions about her family. Perhaps they'd never looked at her properly when she was a teenager—just seen that her grandparents had a "well behaved" girl with them.

The irony almost made her laugh. She'd been prized as much then for slipping into someone else's role as she was now—being the replacement for Grace in Matthew's house. But now wasn't the time for reflection. She had a job to do. She pushed the thoughts aside and smiled, taking the hand of the next wealthy socialite who was being introduced to her.

Matt shook the hand of the man before him, his other hand firmly at Susannah's waist. Since Grace's death, he'd taken his mother anywhere he needed a plus one, so this was strange in some ways. But mainly it felt right. Susannah was a natural—conversing with everyone she met, putting them at ease, finding common ground. He was pretty much following in her wake. She must be great in her role as public-relations manager at the bank she worked for—maybe he should mention her to Laurel, in case his sister was looking for new staff for her PR team at TKG.

And—he smiled inside—if she took a job in Charleston, there would be no need for her to leave his bed. He pulled her a little closer to his side, immeasurably pleased by the idea.

As the couple they'd been talking to moved away, Matt leaned down to speak near Susannah's ear, allowing his lips to brush her lobe. "Thank you for coming tonight."

She shivered and turned her face up to him, her clear blue eyes captivating. "You're welcome."

"Though I'm not sure if I should be thanking you or not for wearing that dress. It's been driving me crazy." He had plans for that dress later. Of peeling her out of it and spending hours exploring the skin it currently covered.

"You chose it," she said sweetly.

Then he saw Larrimore. Dead ahead but walking toward him. He was talking to another man and hadn't seen them yet and by moving a few inches to the right, Matt was able to put himself in their walking path without being too obvious. Subtlety. He was going to play this Susannah's way since he hadn't had any luck with Larrimore so far. Just as the men walked past Susannah's shoulder, he casually looked up and caught the eye of his quarry. The friend walked on, but Larrimore stopped and nodded.

"Mr. Larrimore, good to see you again," he said, extending a hand. "May I introduce you to Susannah Parrish?"

As he spoke the words, Susannah stiffened and leaned back into his hand at her waist, as if her instincts were telling her to get away. The other man's face turned a deep red and he made no move to take Matt's offered hand. Matt dropped it, looking from one to the other, trying to understand the dynamics that had sprung up.

"Parrish?" Larrimore said from between his teeth.

Susannah seemed to be stirred into action by the word—she drew a deep breath and lifted her chin. Then she said one word.

"Grandfather."

Matt's mind reeled. Arnold Larrimore was Susannah's *grandfather*?

The other man grabbed Matt's arm and steered him into a semiprivate alcove. "New plan, Kincaid."

"I'm listening," he said warily, watching Susannah over Larrimore's shoulder. Her face was pale, but she was following them, so he stayed put for the moment.

"That girl broke her grandmother's heart," he said irritably, his eyes reminding Matt of a boxer's in the ring. "You get her to reconcile with my wife and The Kincaid Group gets all Larrimore Industries' business."

Susannah had paused behind her grandfather—close enough to hear, but not to declare her presence. Her eyes were huge in her porcelain face. He remembered her telling him about her grandparents' treatment of her mother, of their underhanded appeals for her to live with them, and of their cruel refusal to help when she needed money for her mother. Her trembling hand lifted to circle her throat, her thoughts plain on her face. She was wondering if he was going to sell her out for the sake of his business.

He glanced back to Larrimore, his heart hardening. "No deal, Larrimore. If your wife—or you—want a relationship with Susannah, you'll have to ask her yourself. But a little friendly advice—she'll probably be more receptive if you ask her directly instead of trying to manipulate her from behind the scenes."

Without waiting for a reply, he reached for Susannah's hand and headed for the door. To hell with subtlety.

Stunned, Susannah allowed herself to be led away. She hadn't expected Matthew to offer her on a platter, but he desperately needed new business for his company. And if he was willing to go out of his way to attend this event tonight just to see her grandfather, then Larrimore Industries would have been a major client for TKG. Under the circumstances, she'd at least expected him to negotiate something more palatable—to look for a win-win.

Yet, here they were, outside the Barclays' mansion, climbing into one of the courtesy cars that would take them to the airstrip where the TKG jet was waiting.

As they settled in the backseat, she laid a hand on Matthew's tense jaw. "Thank you."

"Don't thank me," he said, pulling her closer and tucking her under his arm. "I should have said more to him. Done more."

"What you said was perfect." Utterly perfect. He'd stood up to her grandfather for her—defended her in a way she couldn't remember ever being defended before. Her heart glowed.

"You weren't exaggerating about the old man. To talk about you as if you weren't there, to attempt to trade you like a commodity..." He shook his head, apparently unable to finish the sentence.

She knew she should feel as affronted about her grandfather's behavior as Matthew was. But she didn't. She'd expected no more from him.

Matthew's reaction however...that had been amazing.

Could she give him something of equal value back? If he was prepared to lose the account that he needed for the family business for her, could she put up with visiting her grandparents a couple of times to let him get the deal back? Her body tensed in dissent, but she knew what she had to do. For Matthew.

She pulled away to face him in the dim interior. "I want you to call him and tell him you'll take the deal."

His eyes spat fire. "Like hell I will."

"You need the account," she pointed out.

"Susannah, after he ignored your pleas for money when you and your mother needed him, I wouldn't touch that man's account with a barge pole. But I don't want to talk about him anymore." The car slowed as they reached the airstrip. "We have the night off, my mother is with Flynn and we have the company jet." He stepped out of the car then offered her his hand.

"What do you have in mind?" she asked when they were standing on the tarmac.

The breeze blew her hair around her face and he smoothed it back. "How about I surprise you? Once the pilot gets clearance on a new flight plan, we can go."

She grinned, ready for anything if it involved this man. "Sounds great."

When the jet landed, Susannah had lost track of time. She'd been too absorbed in Matthew and the stories he'd been telling about growing up as one of five children. Seemed the Kincaid kids had been a bit of a handful, but Elizabeth had been more than up to the job.

She peeked out the window; it was hard to see much in the late-night darkness, but they were definitely outside the city area. "Where are we?"

"Willis Hall, not far from Hartsville. My father left it to me."

She turned from the window. "A house with its own airstrip?"

"It's a relatively small strip—the company jet doesn't need as much length as bigger craft. And my grandfather was always fond of cutting out the middleman," he said, unbuckling and picking up his jacket. He'd discarded the cuff links from his dress shirt and rolled up his sleeves to expose his wrists. Ever since she'd first seen those wrists and hands stirring a pot of chili beans, the sight of them made her breath catch. She knew that was an overreaction to a body part, but nothing about her attraction to Matthew had made sense from the day she'd arrived.

The pilot popped around the door. "You're clear to disembark, Mr. Kincaid."

"Thank you, Lachlan," Matthew said, before sliding his arms

into his jacket and guiding Susannah to the door the pilot had opened. They stood for a moment at the top of the steps, looking over toward a grand, two-story antebellum plantation-style house, its tall windows gleaming in the light of the full moon.

She sighed, trying to imagine living in a place so magical for vacations as a child. "Did your father bring you here often?"

"It was my grandfather's vacation home. My mother often brought us out on school holidays to spend time with the extended family. Dad was usually *working*." With the inflection he gave the word "working," it was clear he now thought his father had been with his second family during those holidays. He rubbed a finger across his forehead. "I don't think I've been out in fifteen years."

He climbed down the short set of stairs then turned and held out his hand to help her down—help she appreciated since the steps were harder to navigate in her heels.

On the ground, Matthew took her hand and guided her across the private airstrip toward what looked like a small cottage. "I thought since our night was cut short and Flynn is with Mom, it would be a good time to finally check the place out again."

The night air was cold and quickly seeped through the pink shawl she wore. She shivered and Matthew took off his tuxedo jacket and sat it on her shoulders. His fingers lingered and she shivered again, this time from his nearness.

She looked around at the silhouettes of the trees and stars in the sky, taking in as much as she could discern in the moonlight. If he hadn't been out in fifteen years, then Grace had never been here. A selfish corner of her heart liked that there was something Matthew was sharing just with her.

Though, that also meant Flynn hadn't seen the place. "You didn't come here when you inherited it?"

He shrugged casually. "The will reading was less than two months ago and Flynn was sick with the virus back then. I wouldn't leave him. My PA rang the couple who had been looking after this place and told them to keep doing whatever they'd been doing in the short-term, and I'd continue their salaries. Once things had settled I'd planned to come out and have a look then decide what to do with it."

"What about the pilot?" she asked, glancing back to the plane.

Matthew took out his keys and opened the door to the small building beside the strip. "This staff cottage has been used by pilots and other employees for decades." He flicked a switch and a sitting room was flooded with light. "The couple who look after the house keep it stocked with supplies and entertainments. It's better than the pilot's lounge he was at earlier this evening."

There was a Jeep in a garage beside the cottage, and after taking the key from a hook in the kitchen and snagging a coat for himself from another hook, Matthew guided her to the passenger seat. There was something surreal about coming out to such an isolated spot late at night, and she had to wonder why he'd really suggested it. There must have been other chances for him to check on his inheritance before now.

The short drive, passing the dark shapes of sprawling oaks, was like something from a fairy tale, and when they pulled up in front of an elegant porch, dominated by tall, white Grecian-style columns, she couldn't contain a sigh of wonder.

"Have you thought about what you want to do with the place?" she asked.

"Not really." Instead of climbing out, he turned to face her. "I was close to my grandparents, and when Mom would bring us out on vacations, I was in heaven, just running around and playing all day. I thought I could pass those experiences on to Flynn and make it our vacation home."

He came around to her door and opened it for her and they made their way to the deep front porch. "Then again, maybe I'll sell it," he said as he unlocked the front door.

She looked around at the first room they entered, a large reception room with family portraits in dark frames on cream walls and an assortment of trophies and other mementos on the mantel. "You don't think it's important to keep it in the family?"

"I recently discovered that my father had a different view of what family means than I do." His shoulders rolled back. "So, no, I don't feel a whole lot of obligation about keeping his family's traditions."

The betrayal was still obviously raw for him and she wished there was some way to ease that ache, even though she knew it was something he'd have to work through on his own.

As they walked through the rooms, she was surprised how sparkling and fresh the house was. She'd expected something a little more rustic.

"Your caretakers keep it looking like this all the time?" she asked, turning in a circle.

"Much of it looks the way it did when Grandpa was alive. Since it was only a vacation home, it's always had someone coming in once a week and keeping it ready for the family to drop in."

But one question replayed in her mind. She stopped him with a hand on his forearm. "Matthew, why did you bring me out here tonight?"

"I'm not sure," he said, looking down at her hand as it lay on the dark fabric of his tuxedo coat. Then he laid his large, warm hand over hers, sending sparks dancing across her skin. "I wanted to see it again. And to share that with you."

She bit down on a smile. He genuinely wanted to share this part of himself, of his history, with her. Yet, she could see he was conflicted about his inheritance by the lines that appeared around his eyes. He had a deep attachment to this place, and wanted that for Flynn, but was resisting it because he was still angry at his father. The complexities of this man called to her.

He lifted her hand from his forearm and turned it over, then kissed her palm gently, slowly, and the sweet pressure began to build inside her. He smiled into her eyes—he knew the effect it was having, then he tucked her hand into the crook of his arm.

"There's a sitting room through here with a fireplace," he

said. "I'm hoping part of the caretaker's duties was to keep it ready."

They found the sitting room, with its buttery-yellow walls and dark wood furniture, and Matthew went over to an old wood-burning fireplace that was already packed with kindling and split logs. He found the matches on a nearby ledge and hunkered down to reposition the twigs and scrunched newspaper. The fabric of his black trousers pulled taut over his powerful thighs. As he struck the match, it hissed then caught, and he threw it into the kindling. In the glittering light of the new fire, his cheekbones were accentuated, his profile becoming darkly mysterious.

She moved closer and put her hands out in front of the small flame, welcoming the heat it already generated, wanting to be closer to Matthew's heat, too.

"The house was mainly used in the summer, so fireplaces are all we have for heating," he said, holding his hands out to the warmth, as well.

"You realize I can't see the rest of the house now." She turned, giving her back a chance closer to the flames. "I'm not moving from this fireplace."

The look he gave her heated her skin, even from a distance. "I could be happy with that arrangement." He moved a few paces and took a thick blanket from the back of a chaise longue, then an armload of cushions.

He sauntered back and dropped the cushions haphazardly on the floor and held up the blanket. "I take it that you've heard about the best way to keep warm in the cold?"

"Central heating?"

His mouth twitched. "When there is no central heating."

"Then you might need to explain."

"Body heat." He took her hand and slowly kissed each finger in turn, then the palm. "Clothes off, skin on skin, wrapped in a blanket."

"Are you making a pass at me, Mr. Kincaid?" she asked a little breathlessly.

"No, ma'am." His mouth scorched a path down the inside of her wrist. "I'm solely concerned for your comfort and health."

Her skin flared hotter under his mouth than from the fireplace and, without thinking, she thrust the fingers of her other hand through his short, silky hair. But it wasn't enough. She wanted more.

She tugged her hand away from under his mouth and brought his face up to hers. Pulse soaring, she kissed him hungrily, her lips, her tongue urging him to take what he wanted. He seemed to understand. One hand slid up from her waist, cupping a sensitized breast, gently massaging his way until he found the peak, then brushing it with the back of his hand through the fabric of her dress.

A surge of need overtook her and she shrugged out of his tuxedo jacket, letting it fall to the mess of cushions at their feet and his coat quickly followed.

He reached behind her and unzipped the dress. "You took my breath away in this dress tonight." He pressed an openmouthed kiss to the bare shoulder he uncovered. "But I can't wait another second to see you out of it."

As he slid the fabric down her body and his darkened eyes followed its path, her skin quivered. The desire in his eyes hadn't dimmed from the first time they'd made love. If anything, it increased every time, matching her own growing need for him—each time together offered new opportunities to explore, to create responses, to feel. She couldn't imagine ever tiring of touching his body, of being touched by him.

She worked his shirttails free then unbuttoned the white dress shirt, pushing it over his broad shoulders and down muscled arms. The firelight flickered patterns on his chest, accentuating the ridges of muscle, making the skin shimmer like gold. She ran the pads of her fingers across his collarbone, scraping her nails lightly down his sternum.

"Don't move," she said. "Just give me a few minutes." Matthew was usually so intent on his mission to give her pleasure, and she was normally so absorbed in the sensations he evoked, that she didn't get enough time to tease him the way he teased her.

"Anything you want," he said.

She unbuttoned his trousers, lowering the zipper extra slow, watching his face—his eyes drifted closed and the ridged muscles of his abdomen clenched tight. He held himself completely still, though he was vibrating with the effort of doing it. She hooked her thumbs under the waistband of the trousers and boxers beneath, and lowered them at a leisurely pace, going down on one knee as she took them to his ankles. He lifted one foot then the other so she could slide the shiny shoe and sock off then tug each leg of his trousers away. Still he didn't move.

Her ascent was just as slow, her hands stroking over the rough hairs of his legs, tracing the strong muscles. When she reached the top of his thighs, she wrapped a hand around him and kissed the velvet skin. As he groaned, she felt him sway a little then his knees locked.

"Damn, Susannah," he said through gritted teeth. "You're killing me."

She smiled up at him and found his wallet in the trousers then located the protection she knew he'd have hidden inside. She tore open the wrapper then rolled it slowly over him, placing another delicate kiss at the top. She continued her progress up his body, kissing his abdomen, shaping the curve of his buttocks with her palms, until she was again standing straight.

"I'm all yours," she said with satisfaction, leaning into him.

His eyes flared and, with hands on either side of her head, he kissed her with a primitive hunger. Her heart thumped an erratic beat; her body was drugged by his essence, completely at his mercy.

When he drew away, his breathing was labored and he rested

his forehead on hers. "Thank heavens you were done, because my control was on its last threads."

He wrapped his arms around her and kissed her again. The passion built impossibly fast, and she tugged at the shoulder straps of her bra, wanting, *needing* his touch across all of her skin. Sensing her urgency, he discarded her bra and panties with efficiency, then wrapped the blanket around them both. The musk of his naked skin filled her head, his dark taste was on her tongue, his hard body pressed against hers—he was assaulting her senses on every level. And she wanted everything he had to give.

He pulled her down to the cushions, readjusting the blanket to keep her covered, every movement causing their bodies to slide against each other, driving her to the edge of sanity. Her breath was erratic, too fast to control.

He shifted, pinning her on her back, pressing her into the cushions with a heavy, delicious weight. Desire tugged deep inside her and she arched to meet him, tucking her ankles at the back of his hard thighs. The blanket fell away, but there was no need for it anymore—the heat they were generating rivaled a bushfire. In one long movement, he slid inside her, filling her lusciously, completely, and a deep, wrenching groan was torn from his throat. Yet, as he leaned over her, he stilled, his green gaze locked on her eyes.

"Matthew," she whispered, "this wanting, it's…" She didn't know how to finish, how to describe the overwhelming need she felt for him, all the time.

He flexed his hips and squeezed his eyes shut. "I know," he said in a pained voice. "It's more—you're more—than anything."

He shifted again, and she couldn't think enough to form more words, all she could do was feel the decadence of having him moving inside her. She gripped his shoulders as he increased the pace, arched her hips to meet his long, fluid thrusts, lost herself in the haze of rising pleasure. Rising higher as if she was floating off the floor. His rhythm sending her higher still, out to the clouds, higher. Then his hand reached between them and found the pulsing core of her and she exploded into a thousand fragments, spinning out into the universe, Matthew's name on her lips.

Within moments, he followed her, shouting her name, his movements slowing until he slumped above her, spent.

He rolled to his side, taking her with him, and she rested her head on his heaving chest, clinging to him like a life raft while she found her way back to reality.

When her mind cleared, minutes or hours later, she lay warmed by the fire and his skin, and he pulled the blanket up over her shoulders and tucked her head under his chin. It was a moment so perfect that she dared not move an inch, not wanting to spoil the beauty of it.

Then Matthew stretched, and his fingers drifted down her arm. "Stay," he said against her hair.

The Earth tilted and jarred beneath her as that one word reverberated in her head.

Ten

Susannah stilled. Surely she'd misheard. Misunderstood. "Pardon?"

"Stay with me," he coaxed, pulling her closer. "With me and Flynn."

She went a little dizzy at the thought. If Matthew wanted her with him, could she actually walk away? From the man who made her heart leap whenever she saw him, who ignited a flaming passion deep inside, who was asking her to stay? From the little boy she loved more than life, her own son?

"You said this would be temporary," she said warily. "No illusions, no one would get hurt."

"But it's working. You've fitted into our lives seamlessly, and," he said, his voice lowering, "I like you here."

Her pulse skipped, even though she couldn't afford to be distracted. He thought she'd fitted in seamlessly? Of course she had—she'd been playing a role. Grace's role. "Matthew, I can't see this working out long-term." For more reasons that she could even name.

"Why not? You couldn't be more perfect for Flynn—you love him, I've seen it in your eyes." He lifted her chin with a knuckle. "You're his mother. And things between us are pretty damn fine."

Slowly she sat up, pulling one end of the blanket around her to shield her from the cold—and from the allure of his suggestion. "I can't stay with a man who's still in love with someone else," she said, despite it making her heart ache to say it aloud.

He frowned, then his eyes widened as if he'd realized her meaning and he sat up in a mirror of her pose. "You think I'm still in love with Grace?"

She bit down on her lip, knowing she had to push the point if he was to understand her reasoning. "I can see you are."

"How can you see it?" he asked incredulously.

"Your house is practically a shrine to her." The photos on every wall, her bedroom that hadn't been touched since she died. "And it's in the way you almost flinch every time her name is mentioned. She affects you."

"It's not love," he said tightly, his gaze flicking to the fire. "It's guilt."

Guilt? She hesitated, her brain scrambling to reevaluate everything she knew about Matthew and Grace. "Why would you feel guilty?"

He scrubbed both hands through his hair and turned his face to the ceiling before looking back to her and meeting her gaze. "When Grace died, we were considering a divorce."

Her breath hitched in her throat. Grace and Matthew Kincaid had been talking about a divorce? She wouldn't have believed it if she'd heard it from anyone but Matthew himself. "You seemed like the perfect couple."

"We were college sweethearts and we'd thought back then that what we had would last forever." He rubbed a hand down his face and suddenly looked weary. "But life doesn't always unfold the way you expect it to."

She took his hand. "What happened?"

"Nothing drastic," he said, glancing down at their interlaced fingers. "We married straight out of college. Grace didn't want a job because we'd planned to start a family. But when she didn't become pregnant as soon as she'd hoped, her desire for a baby quickly turned into desperation for one. Maybe not having a job let her dwell on it too much, maybe I didn't support her the way I should have, but it was all she wanted to talk about, all she could think about."

"I knew she was keen, but I hadn't realized it was that strong." Whenever she'd met with Grace, they'd talked about babies, but it had seemed appropriate when their connection was the surrogacy. She hadn't guessed that Grace would be the same everywhere.

"I tried to be understanding—I wanted children, too, and I knew the need was stronger for her. But it took a toll on our marriage. All we talked about was babies, and eventually, we stopped knowing each other. There was no room to talk about our day, or our dreams about anything else." His tone was fairly neutral, but there was a deep pain in his eyes—the hurt from the breakdown of his marriage still lived inside him. "By the time Flynn came along, the damage was done. The only thing we had in common was him. That was enough for the first year, when everything revolved around the baby, but at some point, we realized we were strangers who shared a house and a son."

"Oh, Matthew," she said, her heart bleeding for them both.

"We started to discuss a divorce and even touched on how we'd share custody of Flynn. Then I pushed too far," he said, his voice becoming rough for the first time.

She moved closer, so their knees were touching, wanting to give him as much support as he'd given her so many times over the last few weeks. "Tell me."

"I thought she needed some time away to make sure divorce was what she wanted. I left the house every day for work, but she was home all day, and really only spoke to her parents, me and Flynn. Separating was such a big decision—life changing—

I wanted her to have really thought about it and be sure. For both of us to be sure."

"Grace didn't want to go?" she asked with a sinking feeling in her stomach.

He swallowed hard, then again before continuing. "She was worried because she'd never been away from Flynn for a night. I thought that was even more of a reason for her to have a break. Time to focus on herself and think about our marriage. I'd always been a hands-on father, so Flynn and I would be fine for a weekend."

Her stomach clenched tight. Despite knowing the story had to end badly, part of her still kept hoping Matthew and Flynn could be spared somehow. "I'm almost afraid to ask."

"The TKG jet was already booked, so I chartered a private plane to take her to her parents' place for the weekend and pretty much pushed her out the door." His eyes closed and he pressed fingers to the lids, as if trying to erase the picture in his mind.

She remembered the day she'd returned to Charleston and Matthew had told her Grace had died—he'd said it had happened in a small plane crash. "Something happened to the plane."

"It went down over the water." He flinched, eyes squinting, as if it was happening in front of him. "It took them days to retrieve her body."

She felt physically sick just imagining that day. "Oh, poor Grace."

"She never would have gone if it wasn't for me," he said, his voice a rough whisper. He turned to watch the flickering of the fire and when he turned back, his eyes held more anguish than she'd thought was humanly possible. "It was my idea, I'd chartered the plane, I'd pushed her to go. It was my fault Flynn lost his mother, her parents lost their only child, and a beautiful soul lost her life."

Seeing his naked pain almost made her lose control of the tears that threatened, but he needed her now. She gripped his fingers tight. "Matthew, it was an accident. There's no one to blame. Certainly not you."

"I failed her in the most primal of ways—I didn't protect my wife." His mouth twisted, the skin around his lips so pale. "The only thing I had left to offer her was to keep the secret about being Flynn's biological mother, and to honor her where I could."

"That's why the house feels like a shrine to her." He couldn't bear to move anything away because of the guilt.

He shrugged one shoulder. "For Flynn, too—so he had reminders of her as much as possible."

"You're not still in love with her," she said, finally understanding.

He slowly shook his head. "I wasn't in love with her when she died. I'm sure she wasn't in love with me by then, either."

She wriggled to his side and he wrapped his arms around her. For a long time, neither of them moved more than to give a light caress, neither spoke.

"Stay with me," he whispered.

He was tearing her in two. He might not still be in love with Grace, but he hadn't moved on. Having a temporary relationship with him was one thing, but staying indefinitely? Changing her job and moving interstate for a man who was living in the past and would only ever see her as a replacement for his dead wife? The wife whose death filled him with guilt. Since she'd been in Charleston, she'd been tagging along in Matthew's life like an accessory—attending the Barclays' fundraiser, letting him buy her a dress, drinking fancy wines, fitting into his family's schedule visiting the hospital, cooking family meals. She'd been glad to do what she could, to help. But it had just been the list of tasks that had needed doing. It wasn't about her. It had been the person Matthew had needed her to be, so she'd slotted in.

It was no foundation for a relationship, even if she felt more for him than she'd expected.

She hated society fundraisers, hated being part of the world her grandparents and the Kincaids inhabited—they prioritized money and power, and thought family secrets were par for the course. She couldn't stay in that environment. Yet she couldn't walk away from this man. Or Flynn. What other option was there?

"Tell me, Matthew, what are you really suggesting?"

"If you need a ring to stay, I can do that," he said, the muscles in his neck taut with resistance to the idea.

The blood in her veins turned cold. "You're proposing marriage?" She could barely believe he'd said the words, no matter how reluctantly.

"If you need that," he repeated. "It might be better for Flynn anyway."

Something inside her withered. He thought that she—that any woman—could be happy to be offered marriage "if she needed that"?

"You don't think marriage should be about love and commitment?" Things that would make the union solid and able to weather storms.

"Susannah, I have to be honest. I'm not ready to love again. I don't think I'll ever be ready, but that doesn't change the fact that I want you to stay."

As she looked into his deep green eyes, the pieces finally fitted together. "You don't think you *deserve* love again, do you?"

His eyes slid away. "How about we just keep it simple? You stay with Flynn and me, and we'll all be happy."

Matthew looked down at Susannah's sweet face with no idea what was going on in her head. All he knew was that she was overthinking this. Why fix what wasn't broken? This was working, so they should leave things as they were.

"Matthew, I can't stay."

Before he could answer, his cell buzzed and he reached for his trousers on the floor to find it. The ringtone was the one he'd programmed for immediate family—if one of them was calling this late, it must be important. "We're not finished on this subject," he said as he thumbed the answer button.

"Hello," he said, his eyes still on Susannah as she chewed on her lip.

"Matt, it's Laurel." The tension that vibrated in his sister's voice had him sitting up straight, heart in his mouth.

"Is it Flynn?" Even knowing Laurel wasn't with Flynn tonight, his son was always the first place his mind went when he worried.

"Flynn's fine," she said quickly. "I'm here with him now."

Laurel was at his house late at night—that couldn't be good. "Then where's Mom?"

"The police have taken her in for questioning."

His mother had been taken by the police? His stomach plunged into free fall. "Questioning about what?"

"About Dad's murder," she said, her voice wavering.

His temples began throbbing in a heavy drumbeat. His mother was the last person on Earth who would have anything to do with a murder, let alone her own husband's—surely even the police could see that?

"I'm leaving now," he said reaching for his trousers.

He disconnected and tugged his trousers up his legs. "We have to go back."

"Is your mother in trouble?" Susannah asked, her eyes round and full of concern.

God, he hoped not. But who knew what the justice system would do? "They've taken her in for questioning about Dad's murder."

Her face paled and he offered her a quick reassuring smile. The fire had burned down but he couldn't leave it alight with no one in the house. He looked around and found a fire blanket discreetly hanging in an alcove nearby and ripped it open. Making a mental note to send someone out to replace the safety blanket, he smothered the fire.

Susannah zipped up her dress, frowning. "I've only met your

mother a couple of times, but that sounds crazy. She's not capable of something as violent. As horrific."

"Of course she isn't. Any fool could see that." He grabbed his shirt, shoved his arms down the sleeves and left the sides hang open, unbuttoned. "The detectives are wasting time by interviewing her while the killer walks the streets of Charleston."

He let out an oath as they hurried out the door to the plane.

Susannah followed Matthew through his front door and slipped off her heels. The trip back had been tense and he'd spent much of it on the phone to a lawyer and his siblings. RJ, Kara and Lily were already at the station or on their way, and Matthew's unspoken words were clear—he hated being so far away when his family needed him. She understood. The Kincaids were a family who stuck together and were always there for each other, and yet...they were a family of privilege, secrets and lies. Not a life she could ever be part of.

When they stepped into the parlor, they found a beautiful woman with long, dark auburn hair and green eyes—the picture of Matthew's mother.

"Susannah, this is my sister Laurel," Matthew said brusquely. "Laurel, this is Susannah Parrish."

Laurel held out a hand. "I wish we were meeting under better circumstances, but nice to meet you, anyway." She had tension around her eyes, but her tone was unfailingly polite.

"Likewise," Susannah said, then stepped back to let the siblings talk.

Matthew rubbed the muscles at the back of his neck. "Flynn's asleep?"

"Since before I got here. He won't know anything's happened."

"Thank goodness for small mercies. I don't know why they had to do this at night."

"When I arrived, Detective McDonough and his partner were still here—they'd waited with Mom till she could leave. They said some new evidence had come to light just today, and they were following it up."

"New evidence?" He threw up a hand, palm out. "It's ludicrous to think there could be evidence against her."

Laurel flicked her hair over a shoulder. "I did happen to mention that once or twice."

Matthew showed the first glimmer of a smile since he'd taken Laurel's call. "I bet you did. As I'm sure the lawyers will, too. Have you heard from Mom since they took her?"

"No, but Kara rang when she arrived at the station and said they were all there. Mom's still being questioned. Matt, I—"

He gave a quick nod. "Me, too." He turned to Susannah, reaching for her hand and interlacing their fingers. "Would you mind staying here with Flynn while Laurel and I go down to the police station?"

"Of course I will." She'd been about to offer anyway. "And let me know if there's anything else I can do to help."

He tugged her closer and cupped her cheek with his palm, apparently not caring that Laurel was witnessing the gesture. "Hopefully we won't be long, but even if they drag it out, we should be back before he wakes up."

"Don't worry about me," she said, hoping to at least relieve him of one concern. "We'll be fine. I just hope your mother is okay."

He looked down at her for one beat, then two, the worry for his mother in his eyes, but also the fire that had been there when they'd made love still burned. Then, with no warning, his head swooped down and he kissed her, one hand sliding into her hair, the other behind her back. Helpless, she leaned into him, into the kiss.

Then he pulled back and met her gaze. "Thanks for staying with him."

He turned to Laurel, indicating his rumpled tuxedo with a hand. "I'll just get changed and we'll leave."

He strode for the stairs then took them two at a time, and Susannah dared to peek at Laurel. Matthew had just pretty much announced to his family that they were sleeping together. Now he'd asked her to stay, secrecy was obviously not high on his agenda anymore.

Laurel smiled. "Thank you from me, too."

"Really, I don't mind staying with Flynn."

"Not for that," Laurel said, stepping closer so she could drop her voice. "Matt's my baby brother and he's had a rough time the last few years. Anything that makes him happy gets a ringing endorsement from me."

Susannah felt the blush creep up from her chest to her throat. It was sweet of Laurel to say that but her relationship with Matthew wasn't what Laurel had probably imagined.

She'd be going in a few days, as soon as her leave was up. Despite Matthew's request to stay, there was no way she could.

Matthew came running back down, buttoning a clean shirt as he cleared the stairs, threw a quick kiss on Susannah's cheek, then she was suddenly alone.

She woke on the couch with a start. After a quick shower, she'd been waiting in the parlor for Matthew's return but when she opened her eyes, it was Flynn who stood before her, clutching his favorite teddy, the corners of his mouth turned down.

Fear had her wide-awake in an instant, but she kept her voice calm. "What's the matter, sweetie?"

"I had a bad dream," he said, his bottom lip trembling.

Her chest clenching at his sad little face, she held out her arm and he climbed onto the couch with her, snuggling his warm little back into her chest. She pulled a throw rug from the back of the couch over both of them.

"What was the dream about?" she asked gently.

"I don't mer'ember."

She racked her brain for ideas to deal with childhood bad dreams, but came back to Flynn's own suggestion from when he was in hospital. "Would you like me to sing an Elvis song?"

He nodded, his messy hair brushing under her chin as he did. Holding him a little bit tighter, she sang a verse of "Teddy Bear."

"Sudi?" he said, tipping his head back in an attempt to see her face. "Can I call you Mommy?"

Her heart fell like a stone into her stomach. She and Matthew had tried so hard to be clear with Flynn about her role. Matthew had taken Flynn aside when he first arrived home from hospital and explained that Susannah was only staying temporarily. Then during the week they'd been sure to regularly drop phrases into conversation like, "When Susannah goes home next week," and "During my special little vacation here," to reinforce the message. Obviously their efforts hadn't been clear enough.

Carefully she sat up, bringing him with her, and sat him on her knee. "Sweetie, we've talked about this. You know I'm not your mommy."

"But, maybe you are." His face was serious, as if he'd had an idea that had possibly missed her notice.

She was almost afraid to ask, but forewarned was forearmed. "Why would you think so?"

"You live in our house," he said, his solemn eyes barely blinking.

"I don't really live here. I'm just staying for a little vacation." Though she knew that distinction might be lost on a three-year-old.

Undeterred, he pressed on. "You cook for us like a mommy."

"That's only because your daddy can't cook. In some families, it's the daddy who cooks. And in your family, Pamela makes most of your meals, doesn't she?"

Reluctantly he nodded. Then he perked up. "Daddy kisses you like a mommy."

She could have slapped herself. They thought they'd been so careful, not kissing anywhere Flynn could see them. Apparently their attempts at being discreet had failed.

Although, perhaps Flynn had been on the lookout as he collected his list of evidence. Now his list encompassed that she kissed like a mommy, sang like one, cooked like one, lived in their house and kissed the daddy.

And the worst part was he was *right*.

She'd slipped into the role of wife and mother so easily. But it wasn't *her* role. And neither Kincaid saw her as anything more than that role.

"I think it's time we put you back to bed," she said, moving him onto the couch beside her. "You can talk about this tomorrow with your dad."

His smile drooped and it broke her heart. Everything inside her wanted to say that she would be his mommy. That she *was* his mommy.

But Flynn deserved a mother who had a proper relationship with his father, where there was love and marriage and plans of forever. It was the only way to create a secure family unit for the little boy. One day Matthew would be ready to move on, and he'd find the perfect mother for Flynn. But Matthew wasn't ready yet and, therefore, it wasn't her.

Now she just had to tell Matthew.

Eleven

When Matthew finally arrived home from the police station, the sun was peeking over the horizon. Dark circles underlined his eyes and his every movement conveyed exhaustion. Susannah walked over to where he was closing the door behind him, her entire body vibrating with tension about what she would have to say, knowing she would be adding to the stress lining his face.

He pulled her into an embrace, slumping a little of his weight onto her shoulders, and let out a deep sigh. She wanted nothing more than to take him upstairs and hold him while he slept, but that was not on the agenda—now or ever. She closed her eyes and saw Flynn's little face, solemnly asking if he could call her Mommy. This couldn't wait. So she simply held him in her arms, and wished things could be different.

He straightened and yawned and she stepped back, folding her arms tightly under her breasts. "How's your mother?"

"Tired. Upset." He speared his fingers through his short hair. "But they've finished questioning her and Laurel's taking her home."

She had only met Elizabeth a couple of times but she'd liked her, and hated to think of her going through something so awful—being questioned at a police station, being a suspect in a murder investigation, or the horror of knowing your husband had been murdered. She repressed a shiver.

"Have they eliminated her from suspicion now?"

"I'm not sure what they've decided. Our lawyers have told us not to worry, which is a little hard to achieve. Detective Mc-Donough told Mom not to leave town while they further their investigations. Which could mean they still suspect her, or could have been a parting shot to keep us all on our toes."

"Matthew," she said, then paused to moisten her lips, "I'm sorry about the timing, but there's something important I need to tell you."

He checked his watch then glanced at the window where the sun's first rays were shining. Turning back to her, he opened his mouth and she knew he was about to ask if it could wait, but something of her anguish must have shown on her face because he rubbed his eyes and said, "Sure, shoot."

Part of her wanted to jump at the reprieve he'd been about to offer, to delay the inevitable heartache, but that would be cowardly and only make things worse for Flynn. For everyone. "Thank you. It's already waited too long."

His eyes were wary as they regarded her, then he nodded. "This looks like a conversation I'll need to pay attention to. Let me get a coffee first." He headed through to the kitchen and asked, "Do you want one?" over his shoulder.

She was already wired enough without the caffeine. "No, thanks."

Belly churning, she watched his hands work efficiently and methodically filling the machine with coffee grounds before turning it on. His eyes were preoccupied, weary, and she remembered this was a man who'd lost his wife and father in a twelve-month period, whose son had suffered a major illness, and whose mother had as good as been accused of murder. And now she was about to add to his burden. *I'm sorry, Matthew.*

Once his mug was full and steaming, he leaned back against the counter and drank. Then he leveled his gaze at her. "Is this about our conversation at the farmhouse?"

"No." She felt a tear escape and roll down her cheek. "And yes."

"Hey," he said, setting his mug down and pulling her against his chest. "What's happened?"

You happened, she wanted to say. *My life was fine then Flynn fell sick and you called me and now nothing's the same.* Despite Flynn's health improving, it was too late—she'd been drawn into their lives and could barely see a way out past the entanglements, past the caring.

She rested her cheek against his chest and focused on the half-empty mug on the counter beside them. "Flynn woke during the night and we had a talk."

He lifted her chin with his thumb, his eyes one hundred percent alert now. "What kind of talk?"

"He's been collecting more evidence that I'm his new mother," she said, trying not to wince as she remembered Flynn's earnest little face.

Matthew's arm stiffened around her. "What's he got?"

"I live here, I cook and—" she drew in a trembling breath "—I kiss the daddy."

He closed his eyes and swore. "I had no idea he'd seen us."

"Matthew, it's gone too far. Flynn's already going to be disappointed when I leave. I have to go today, before he can ask again."

He shook his head, dismissing the idea. "Flynn wants you to stay—that only strengthens my case." He kissed her cheek, the tip of her nose. "You fit in here. Stay with us."

How easy it would be to say yes, to stay here forever, to lose herself in their lives. She knew she couldn't stay as a replacement, but her heart ached to do exactly that, despite the price....

She couldn't think straight in his arms—the very reason she'd become so entangled in his life in the first place. Calling on every ounce of willpower she possessed, she extracted herself from his embrace and leaned back against the opposing counter. The cool air stung her skin where Matthew's body heat had warmed her only seconds ago.

"The thing is I fit in here a little *too* well."

"How can you fit in too well?" he asked, his eyes narrowing.

She swallowed, trying to moisten her parched throat. "It's like you and Flynn have just been waiting for someone to fill the Grace-shaped hole in your family. I tick all the boxes—there's an attraction between us, I'm Flynn's biological mother, I cook."

He snorted. "How can it be a bad thing that we meld together as a family?"

She wrapped her arms around her middle and held herself tight as if she could stop herself from falling to pieces in front of him. "Because when I eventually have a family of my own, it will be somewhere I'm wanted for *myself.*" Her eyes were stinging, and she tried to stop the tears from forming. "My worth in this house is primarily as a replacement."

His eyes widened. Blazed. "That's ridiculous."

"I know you didn't mean it to happen this way, and that it's partly my fault, but neither of you know *me.*" Was it so wrong to want to be seen for herself? Wanted for herself? She cast around for a way to explain. "When people start a relationship, or a family, it's like the edges of their joining are elastic, and they move out around the things both people bring to that relationship. But nothing changed here. I fitted in the spaces that were already vacant. There's nothing about me here."

"That's crazy, Susannah. To start with, your desserts were new," he said with a little grin.

"Grace cooked, Pamela cooked." She lifted one shoulder and let it drop again. "I continued the tradition. That my dishes were different hardly matters."

He scrubbed his fingers through his hair, frustration shining in his eyes. "I don't even know what you're talking about. I *know* you're not Grace."

Her bottom lip quivered but she wouldn't let the emotion overtake her, not until she was on her own. "I don't think anyone here can be sure of what they know," she said slowly. "Everything is smoke and mirrors—you're living in the past because you can't let go of your guilt, your father had secrets, you have secrets. I'll bet there are other secrets in your family yet to come out."

His eyes hardened. "You know why I can't tell people about Flynn. I swore to Grace I wouldn't tell a soul. And even if I could break it, her parents would be destroyed if they found out—all it would take would be one person who knows to slip up. You and I are as far as the information can ever go."

"I do, Matthew, I understand." She could feel the tears that welled in her eyes begin to spill over, and she swiped at them. "But you have to understand that I need to leave today, both for my own sake and for Flynn—before he gets any more attached."

He grabbed his mug and cast the remains of his coffee down the sink, then turned to face her again, hands low on hips. "So you're just walking away? From Flynn?"

Had he forgotten what he'd asked of her? Nothing as simple as taking another week's leave. He'd asked her to confront a mother's deepest instinct and decide whether she'd stay with the son she'd borne. Yes, she'd originally felt the baby had been his and Grace's, but that was before she'd spent time with Flynn.

"I have to, Matthew," she whispered, suddenly cold all over. "Please don't make this harder."

He raised his eyebrows pointedly. "If it's hard, then maybe it's wrong."

She squeezed her eyes shut—she couldn't do this anymore. Couldn't keep discussing why she had to go. It hurt far too much.

"I'll say goodbye to Flynn this morning," she said, looking

out the window. "And I'll send him a couple of letters and presents from Georgia so the cut isn't too abrupt."

"What about me?" he asked bitterly. "How are you going to ease the break for me?"

"The same way I'll ease it for myself. Time." She choked in a breath. "I'll miss you, Matthew." She couldn't deny it, even if she wanted to.

His face softened, and he pulled her roughly against him. "I'll miss you, too."

She melted into him and for the last time, just let herself feel him against her. Let herself smell the scent of his skin through his shirt. Feel the day-old stubble against her temple. He leaned down and gave her a lingering kiss that tasted of coffee but felt like sadness. She needed to pull away, yet she couldn't make herself. And then she realized why.

She'd gone and fallen in love with him. Her stomach swooped low.

He was right. If it was hard, then it was probably wrong—it *shouldn't* be easy to leave the man you loved. But it only made things worse. It was an unrequited love—Matthew had made no secret of the fact that he'd never let himself love again. If she'd been the woman to change his stance, he'd have changed it already.

And, even if he could love her, Matthew didn't see her, the real her. If she stayed, she'd forever be living Grace's life, not her own. A life as a Kincaid in a world she'd escaped once as a teenager.

Drawing a shaky breath, she pulled away and dashed for her bedroom to pack. Hot tears streamed down her face freely. If she didn't go today, she might settle for this half life and stay forever.

A few hours later, Matt watched Susannah climb into a taxi in his driveway, his chest ripping open. Everything was good with her here—they fitted together, their strengths complemented each other, he couldn't imagine he'd ever have enough of her in his bed and Flynn adored her.

But that wasn't enough for this woman. Susannah Parrish wanted it all. More than he had to give. His temples pounded. He'd given his heart away once and it had been decimated when things had collapsed between him and Grace. Realizing they'd fallen out of love, that all his dreams of the future for his marriage and their little family were gone, had been almost more than he could bear. He'd never offer his heart again.

And Susannah wouldn't settle for anything less.

When she'd stood up to his brothers at the hospital, he'd admired her refusal to back down, her stubbornness. And though he was desperate to make her stay, a little part of him still had to admire her commitment to what she wanted.

Flynn was inside with his grandmother. He'd cried when they told him Susannah was leaving, but the promise of postcards and presents from Georgia had mollified him somewhat. The taxi crawled down the driveway and paused before turning onto his quiet street. Susannah looked up and he caught her gaze. Her face was pinched as she refused to let herself cry. Damn it. *Why was she doing this?*

She thought he didn't see her? Every time he closed his eyes, it was her smile that appeared. She'd invaded his dreams at night, his thoughts during the day. How could she think he didn't see her?

The taxi moved off down the street and he forcefully locked away everything he was feeling. He couldn't afford to fall apart—he had a little boy depending on him.

He thumbed the keyless lock on his car, climbed in and headed for the TKG building. The first order of business was to explain to RJ why he'd lost the Larrimore's account last night. Not something he'd been looking forward to, but compared with Susannah leaving, it no longer seemed to matter as much.

He picked up two coffees from their favorite coffee shop on

the way, wishing it was late enough in the day for Scotch instead.

"Good morning, Brooke," he said to RJ's secretary. "Is my brother in?"

Brooke looked up from her computer screen and smiled. "Good morning, Matthew. I just took him a pile of papers to sign, so he'll probably be glad for the interruption."

RJ was sitting at his desk and stretched his arms over his head when Matt knocked on the open door. "You've come bearing gifts. Excellent."

Matt walked across to the desk and put a steaming cup of coffee in front of him. "Thought we could use the extra caffeine today."

RJ had been at the police station by the time Matt had arrived last night, and had probably had as much sleep as he'd had—none.

"Have you spoken to Mom today?" RJ asked after taking a sip of the dark brew.

Matt nodded. "She's at my place. She's still a little shaken, but seems fine. She insisted on staying with Flynn to give her something to do."

Matt never would have asked her to do it—he'd have preferred to keep her wrapped up in cotton wool today. Perhaps send her off to a spa to be spoiled for a few hours. But his mother had rung early and insisted looking after Flynn was what she wanted. She said seeing Flynn healthy put everything else that was going on into perspective.

RJ put the coffee on his desk and frowned at it. "She was with him last night when they took her in, wasn't she?"

Matt nodded. Time to come clean. "I went to the Barclays' fundraiser. Which is what I need to talk to you about."

"You were hoping to tie things down with Larrimore, weren't you?"

Matt's blood simmered thinking about Larrimore's offer last night to deliver Susannah in exchange for the account. He should have said or done more, but at the time, his first priority had been getting Susannah out of there. He took a swig of his coffee and drained the cup. The next time he met the old man, things would be different. He had no idea what he'd do, but someone needed to bring the man down a peg.

He crumpled his empty cup and pitched it into the wastebasket. "The deal's off the table."

RJ swore. "Did he give a reason for canceling?"

"I ended it," Matt said evenly, confident he'd done the right thing.

RJ's jaw dropped. "Why the hell did you do that?"

"Turns out Larrimore is Susannah's grandfather. Due to some history between them, she's estranged herself." Rightly so—the man was a bully. And Matthew would never let anyone hurt Susannah, grandfather or not, potential client or not. "When he saw her with me last night, he offered a new deal—I get Susannah to make nice and we get their business."

"You sided with her," RJ surmised, raising his brows.

"Beyond the point that I'm not willing to manipulate people to get an account, she had a solid reason for estranging herself in the first place."

"You're pretty tight with this Susannah. What's your plan there?"

Despite his heart beating like a freight train, Matt schooled his features to be neutral. "No plan. She's gone."

"That surprises me," RJ said, leaning back and interlocking his fingers behind his head. "That day at the hospital, there was definitely something between you."

Something? What had sparked with Susannah had been more than something, more than he could have dreamed. A tidal wave of anguish threatened to crash over him and he steeled himself against its power. "There might have been, but it's over."

"Is this about Grace? You're still hooked on her?"

Matt looked up sharply. Seemed Susannah wasn't the only one who'd thought that. He heaved out a breath. He owed his brother the truth. "Grace and I were talking about a divorce when she died."

RJ dropped his arms and sat up straight. "Lord. I had no idea."

"She was going away for the weekend to think about it." The guilt still burned in his gut, but the story was a little easier told a second time. Had lost the sharpest edges, thanks to Susannah's gentle listening. "We had to make sure it was what we really wanted."

RJ's head tilted to the side, his eyes incredulous. "All this time I thought you'd put your life on hold because you were still in love with her."

Matt frowned. "What do you mean, I'd put my life on hold?"

"You walk around like, I don't know, your insides are bound tight or something." RJ winced, clearly uncomfortable, but willing to proceed anyway. "The only time there seems to be a spark of life in you is when you're with Flynn. Kara said to me once that your eyes say you're closed for business."

It's like you and Flynn have just been waiting for someone to fill the Grace-shaped hole in your family.

Waiting.

The room closed in on him until he couldn't breathe. He ran a finger around the collar of his shirt. *Had* he put his life on hold? Waiting for...waiting for what?

Abruptly he stood and headed for the watercooler in the corner of RJ's office and poured himself a drink. Susannah had accused him of thinking he didn't deserve to love again. Deep down, he knew that was true to some extent. But added to that, he could see that because Grace died when they were talking about a divorce, he'd never had closure. He'd been in limbo about the end of their relationship.

He'd been unable to grieve his wife as a man in love, and hadn't been granted divorce papers the way a man leaving a relationship would. With neither avenue open, he'd stood still. Stagnant.

He turned to find his brother watching him warily. "I really have had my life on hold, haven't I?"

RJ nodded, clearly relieved the awkward part of the conversation was over. "Have you opened the letter Dad left you yet?"

When their father's will had been read, they'd all been handed a letter their father had written. Each of Reginald's five children, his wife, his mistress and his mistress's two sons. Matt had watched RJ open his straightaway but he simply couldn't bring himself to do the same. He'd been too angry. If his father had been standing in front of him instead of lying in his grave, he'd have walked away, too angry to talk to him—he hadn't wanted to talk to him via a letter, either.

He rubbed his fingers across his forehead. Maybe it was time he gave his father a hearing.

"I'll catch you later," he said to his brother on the way out the door.

Back in his office, Matt slid open the second drawer of his desk and reached below the papers there to find the envelope he hadn't seen since the day his father's will had been read. He hadn't wanted the letter at his house, in his private life, so he'd thrown it at the bottom of this drawer and tried to forget about it.

But despite his anger at his father, it was time to read the man's final words to him.

Dear Matthew,

I hesitate to write this letter, because I know of all my children, you'll be the most disappointed in me. And perhaps you have the right to judge me harshly. You know how hard it is to be a father, how much we want to do the best by our children, how we want to give them the world.

The difference between us is you've become a better father to Flynn than I could ever have hoped to be to any of my children. In the short time you've had that little boy, you've devoted yourself to him, then, after losing Grace, you've been all things to your son.

I'm proud of you. More proud than I could say to your face. You've become a fine man, a good father.

I wish I'd been half the father to you, to all my children, that you are to Flynn. I've failed Jack the worst, but I've kept this secret from you all these years, and left you to find out after I've gone.

All I can ask for now is forgiveness. I have no excuses. All I can offer is my apology and to tell you that if you can't forgive me, I'll understand. And that I'll still love you and be proud of you.

Love,
Dad

A great, thick ball of emotion clogged his throat, and he struggled to get control. This hadn't been what he'd expected. If he'd thought about what was in the letter at all, he'd have predicted a bunch of excuses and a request to play nice with Jack and Alan.

Instead it was full of love and...and admiration. The grief he'd put a stopper on since the day of the will reading burned the backs of his eyes. But he was no role model for fatherhood. He'd just screwed up again by letting Flynn get attached to Susannah then scaring her off.

Susannah.

She'd said it was all smoke and mirrors with him. His father had secrets and he'd had secrets. She was right.

He'd been angry at his father for not telling them that he'd fathered a child before he'd married their mother, yet here he was, keeping Flynn's biological mother a secret.

He stalked to the window, leaning an arm on the frame.

"I'm sorry, Grace," he whispered to the white clouds hovering over Charleston, "but I can't do it anymore. I can't let Flynn grow up with secrets, too."

To be the man his father had thought he was, he had to step

up to the plate. He needed to tell his family that Susannah was Flynn's biological mother, and she needed to be there to hear it. To be acknowledged by them.

In three strides, he was back at his desk, phone in hand. He dialed Susannah's cell and waited. She should have touched down in Georgia by now. How would she react to hearing from him again, and so soon? Would she refuse to come? His pulse resounded in his ears.

It rang five times before she picked up, which gave him a few moments to plan what he wanted to say. But when he heard her voice, the sweet sound flowed around and through him and his mind froze. All he could think about was her blue eyes, the way her blond hair would be falling around her shoulders, her lips parted to say his name.

Susannah stood in the hall outside her apartment, keys in one hand, her carry-on suitcase in the other, her cell phone wedged between her shoulder and ear as she tried to unlock the door.

"Hello?" she repeated. She should have checked the display screen when she answered, but her hands were full and she was in a rush to get inside, so she'd just thumbed the answer button.

It had been a horror flight home. The plane had traveled smoothly, but she'd spent the entire time praying she'd made the right decision, knowing she'd spend the rest of her life convincing herself she'd done the right thing to leave Matthew. To leave Flynn. The key turned in the lock and she pushed through, but still the person on the other end of the phone didn't speak.

"Hello?" she said again, dropping her suitcase and shutting the door. She was about to hang up, when a voice familiar and dear said her name.

Her heart clenched and twisted. "Matthew." Then her brain caught up. "Is it Flynn? Has something happened?"

"He's fine. He's home with my mother."

"Oh, thank God," she said, relieved beyond measure.

"But I would like you to come back to Charleston for something."

She squeezed her eyes shut and leaned against the back of her couch. If he asked her to go back to him, would she have the strength to refuse again?

"Matthew—" But he interrupted her.

"I can't let Flynn grow up with secrets," he said, his voice firm. "I'm going to tell my family that Grace wasn't his biological mother. That you are. And I'd like you to be there when I tell them."

Stunned, she moved to the front of the couch and sank down into the overstuffed cushions. "Why?"

"I think it's only fair that you're acknowledged when I tell them."

"No, why are you telling them at all? You said you could never break that vow to Grace."

"My obligations to Flynn outweigh my responsibility to Grace. I have to do what's right by him, and the right thing is for him to know everything as soon as he's ready."

He was really going to tell them. Then tell Flynn when the boy was ready.

Flynn would always know she was his biological mother.

A flower of hope, of love, bloomed in her chest, but before it became too big, she needed to close it down. Exposing this secret would make everything so much more complex. How would Flynn feel? Would it make things harder for him, to have another mother who didn't live with him and his daddy? Would Matthew want her to keep in touch with Flynn? And where would that leave her relationship with Matthew—it had been hard enough to walk away once, could she do it over and over?

She pinched the bridge of her nose, trying to make sense of her swirling thoughts, and of Matthew's change of heart. "That must have been a hard decision."

"Not once I had a couple of things pointed out to me." His

voice was almost rueful, yet the tension it held was too strong for that.

She knew she had no right to ask, but until a few hours ago, she'd been privy to his innermost thoughts, so the words tumbled out. "By who?"

"You. RJ. My father," he said, and before she could question how he'd had advice from his father, he asked, "Will you come?"

Could she do it? *Should* she? Walk back into the Kincaids' world for a day. Be near the man she loved but couldn't have. Be acknowledged as the mother of a little boy she loved, but would never be a proper mother to.

Once this information came out, she and Matthew would need time to discuss the ramifications, and plan how they wanted to handle the future for Flynn, so she guessed they'd have to meet at some point, anyway.

Weary and overwhelmed, she rubbed her eyes with a trembling hand. "When are you going to tell them?"

"This Sunday. My family has lunch together every Sunday, so they'll all be there. In fact, it'll be the first time I've been since Flynn went to hospital."

She could think of nothing worse than facing the Kincaids when they learned she was the biological mother of their grandson and nephew. Memories crowded in—her grandparents' displeasure at everything she did. The agony of facing the family of the boy she'd been pregnant to as a teenager. How overpowered she'd felt. She lifted her chin. She was a different person now. This time she would stand up, not only for Matthew, but for Flynn and herself.

To get her voice to work, she had to swallow hard. "I'll be there."

She disconnected and—once again—hoped to heaven she'd done the right thing. For all their sakes.

Twelve

As he waited for Susannah at the airport arrivals gate for the second time in a month, Matt found himself tapping his thighs with his thumbs, nervous as all hell. It had only been a matter of days since he'd seen her last, yet it felt like an eternity. His arms were desperate to hold her, to keep her here by his side.

At three in the morning as he'd lain awake, aching for her, optimism had surfaced and he'd wondered if she missed him this much, too. If her torment was half as strong as his, maybe she'd reconsidered and would stay this time.

She emerged through the door; the long blond hair that had curtained their faces when she'd leaned down to him was around her shoulders. The lips that had scorched his body were painted blush-pink and pressed together in a flat line. The crystalline-blue eyes that had darkened with passion when she looked at him were searching the crowd.

She was carrying a large handbag. Not the small carry-on suitcase she'd had last time—she really was planning to return to Georgia tonight. His stomach withered as disappointment surged.

When her gaze landed on him, he stilled, looking for a clue as to her thoughts. She gave away none beyond some nerves of her own in the way she touched her hair. He made his way over and kissed the silken skin of her cheek. Two inches to the right of where he wanted to kiss, but she'd withdrawn the right.

"Did you have a good flight?" he asked, annoyed that his voice sounded more like a rasp.

"Yes, thank you."

So formal. This woman who'd loved his body with such passion. The contrast between what they'd had and how things now stood between them was gut-wrenching. He placed a hand at the small of her back and guided her to the exit nearest his car.

Just outside the door, her step faltered. She looked up at him, a small line between her brows. "Matthew, I've been thinking about Grace's parents since you rang. If you tell everyone about me, then how will they…?"

He guessed her mind. He'd been worried, too. "I've told them." It had been important to him that they hear before his own family. "I visited them yesterday and told them everything. About how devastated Grace had been about not having a child of her own blood, and why she'd wanted all the details of the egg donation to be kept secret. How devoted she'd been to Flynn and how proud they could be of her. And how much Flynn loves them." He hadn't wanted doubts on any of these points.

"How did they take it?"

"There were tears," he admitted as they threaded their way through lines of parked cars. "But I think after they get over the shock they'll be okay. I explained that they would always be Flynn's grandparents, and I had no intention of restricting their access. They're too important to Flynn to ever jeopardize that."

"You're a good man, Matthew Kincaid," she said quietly.

He swore under his breath. A good man, but not good enough to stay with. She still believed the ridiculous idea that she was a replacement for Grace, and nothing he said seemed to convince her otherwise.

They arrived at his car and he opened the passenger door for her. She stepped in and he closed the door.

As he slid into the driver's seat, she said, "You might be interested to know that I had a call from my grandmother last night."

He paused before starting the ignition. "Did you take the call?"

"Against all my instincts," she said with a little smile, and some of the strain between them melted away.

"Then why answer it?"

She paused, tucking her hair behind her ears. "Remember what my grandfather said at the Barclays'?"

"That you broke your grandmother's heart." It had been a low blow and Matt was still furious thinking about it. He reached for her hand and held it between his. "If you ask me, they reaped what they sowed."

"Maybe," she said, looking down at their joined hands. "But my father put up with his parents because he believed in forgiveness. And he must have loved them, too."

"If he'd stood up to them sooner, you might not have had to endure their control games and manipulations."

"From what my grandmother said—and didn't say—I think I might have been the first person to stand up to them. They're rich, they have social position and my grandfather is a bully. People have let them get away with a lot."

"But not you." His chest swelled, he was so incredibly proud of her in this moment.

She gave him a beautiful smile, obviously picking up on the genuine emotion in his voice. "We might be able to come to a new understanding." Her smile faded and her gaze was earnest as it met his. "Another thing she said was that she wasn't happy with the deal my grandfather put to you at the Barclays', and to

make up for it, she told Granddaddy to give Larrimore Industries' business to your company. He'll be calling you tomorrow."

He couldn't help the grin that spread across his face. "I'd
have liked to have been a fly on the wall when she told him to
do that. I think I'll enjoy taking his call." Not wanting to lose
the more relaxed mood, an idea formed in his head. "We've got
a bit of time before the family lunch, and Flynn is already there
with Mom and Pamela. Is there anything you want to do?"

"How much time do we have?"

He checked his watch. "About an hour, give or take."

She bit down on a smile. "Have you heard of John's Point?"

He hadn't been to the little lookout for years, and couldn't
see any particular appeal for a visit. He'd hoped she'd suggest
somewhere more private. Intimate. But she was here today at
his request, so the least he could do was drop by if she wanted
to see it.

"Sure," he said and started the car.

They spent the drive talking about Flynn's health and the
Elvis songs he'd conned people into singing recently. In the days
since Susannah had left, Matt had missed many things about her,
but this kind of easy conversation was perhaps one he'd missed
the most.

When they arrived at the small viewing platform on the rocky
outcrop, her eyes lit up and the effect was mesmerizing. She
undid her seat belt and climbed out before he could get around
to open her door.

"What is it about this place?" he asked as he clicked the keyless lock.

The wind whipped her hair around her face. "When I was a
girl, my father used to bring me here."

She began to climb the path and he followed behind. "So it
reminds you of your father?"

"Yes." She turned and looked at him over her shoulder, grinning. "And no."

Matthew chuckled. They reached the top, a little-known lookout with a panoramic view over Charleston and out to sea. "You like the view?"

"Sure, the view's great," she said over her shoulder.

He could live an entire life with Susannah Parrish and never tire of trying to figure out what was going on in her mind. "That's not why you wanted to come."

"Nope," she said and walked to the rail and stretched out her arms. The strong wind smoothed the hair from her face, pressed her dress against her curves. Her eyes drifted closed and her mouth tugged wide in a smile of deep pleasure.

"I used to come here often when I lived in Charleston," she said, her eyes still closed. "Every week, if I could manage it."

"You came for the wind," he said, as it finally made sense. He remembered the look of joy on her face that morning in his courtyard. "You have a thing for the wind."

"I do," she said without embarrassment. "It revitalizes me. Some people like adrenaline sports, some like the water. I like the breeze in my hair, against my skin."

"I have to admit, I like seeing you with the breeze in your hair." She was magnificent. Like a goddess.

She opened one eye and smiled at him. "Come and try it." She held out a hand and without thinking, he took it, stepping up onto the bottom rung of the railing, and leaning forward so it took his weight. She moved behind him and lifted his arms to the side before taking up her own position again.

"Now close your eyes," she said, not looking at him. "And pretend you're alone with the breeze."

Feeling a little foolish, he followed her instructions and was amazed to find that within seconds, the world faded away and almost his entire focus was taken by the current of air that pressed against him. *Almost* his entire focus. Because he never lost the awareness of Susannah. He reached out his fingertips and found her hand, entangling them together. Hers didn't respond at first, then they quickly wrapped around his, tightly. He opened his eyes and glanced over. She was looking at him and he could see straight into her heart, and he finally understood something in his conscious mind that he had always known, soul deep.

Susannah was no woman's replacement.

She'd been right that he had seen her that way on some level. He'd used it as a defense against falling in love with her because he couldn't stand the thought of things going the same way they had with Grace. But nothing with Susannah would go the same way, because Susannah was nothing like Grace. Whatever happened between them would be unique and belonging to them alone.

He wanted that. Wanted everything that came of being with her.

"Susannah," he said, his voice rough with all he hadn't said.

"No, Matthew. Please don't say it again. I can't stay." Her eyes filled with tears. Tears he'd caused.

Everything inside him wanted to rise up and revolt, to refuse to accept. But no matter how many times he asked, she kept giving the same answer. He wouldn't beg, and even if he did, he doubted it would make any difference.

He dropped his arms and straightened. Despite the canyon-size ache inside, he had to keep himself together or he'd never get through the next few hours with his family.

He checked his watch. "It's probably time we got to my mother's."

The drive to the Kincaid mansion was silent. Why had she done something as foolish as take him to John's Point? At the airport, things had been too formal, almost abrupt. But they'd settled in to being able to carry a conversation. Then she'd ruined that and could kick herself for making things more difficult for him just before he had to confront his family.

They pulled up in front of an elaborately embellished Federal mansion with a gorgeous porch and outbuildings to the side.

While she gaped at the beauty of the building, Matthew came around and opened her door.

A swarm of butterflies fluttered in her belly. What would his family think of her? Would they judge her to be good enough to be the mother of their precious nephew and grandson? They'd seemed to like her when she was a friend, but things would be different now. This was Flynn's family, and despite having met most of them before, she wanted to do the right thing. Make the right impression, for Flynn's sake.

Matthew took her hand as she stepped out, and guided her in with a warm palm at the small of her back. As they walked through the door, her gut clenched tight. Suddenly she was alone. And small. Just like when she was a child visiting her grandparents or accompanying them to their friends' homes. Big, impressive houses where the cream of society lived.

People waiting to judge her and find her lacking.

Noises floated on the air from a room farther away—a large family laughing, talking, glassware clinking. She was reminded of her mother visiting the Larrimores' for the first time—the beginning of their campaign of exclusion and snubbing.

Matthew leaned down to her ear, his breath warm as it feathered over her cheek. "Everything okay?"

She looked up into his brilliant green eyes and the world tilted to correct itself and she was back to being herself again. "Everything's fine," she said.

Except that she'd never have him. Another difference between her arrival here and her mother's at the Larrimore mansion became clear—her father had been besotted and had proposed with romance and genuine passion. Matthew had offered her a ring "if she needed it." The ache inside was almost unbearable. She shut it away—dwelling on it wouldn't change a thing, it would only make today harder to live through.

They entered a large, exquisitely decorated room and Elizabeth and RJ smiled as they came over to greet her. Matthew introduced her to Lily and her fiancé, Daniel, then Kara and

Laurel came into the room, glasses of iced tea in their hands, deep in conversation. They saw her and came over to kiss her cheek, both with mischievous grins—Laurel had obviously told Kara about the kiss she'd witnessed the night Elizabeth had been taken in for questioning.

Elizabeth slid her hand in the crook of Matthew's arm. "You said you had something to tell us?" Her eyes were wide, hopeful, and Susannah had a bad feeling. His family thought this was going to be a happy announcement, perhaps even an engagement...

"I do. Where's Flynn?"

Elizabeth waved an arm toward the door. "In the kitchen house with Pamela. She'll keep him out there till we come for him."

"Thanks." Susannah saw the tension lurking in his eyes when he glanced at her, but his face was calm and composed when his gaze returned to his family. "Perhaps if we all sit down?"

"Shall I get the champagne?" Laurel asked.

Matthew winced, finally understanding their expectations, and his shoulders seemed to take on an even heavier weight. "It's not that sort of news."

There were some rumblings in the group. "Then what the hell kind of news is it?" RJ asked, clearly speaking for them all.

"Let's go in here," Matthew said, indicating the less-formal family room. Buzzing with curious anticipation, his family filed in, sitting on couches, Kara on the corner of a coffee table, RJ on the armrest of one couch.

"There's something I should have told you before now," he began. His shoulders were tense. Standing a few feet to the side of him, Susannah knew this was tearing him up inside because he felt he was betraying Grace, but he was going to do it, anyway. Because he thought it was the right thing to do. She'd never loved him more. She wanted to lace her fingers through his to offer support, but knew it would give the wrong impression to his family, and they were already suspicious more existed between Matthew and her than friendship.

Instead she moved an infinitesimal step closer and he looked up. She gave him an encouraging smile, and some of the tension melted from his features.

He turned back to his family. "You all know Grace was unable to carry a baby to term. What you don't know is that Susannah was the surrogate who carried Flynn."

There were a couple of gasps, and a few comments about not having told them sooner, but he continued on. "There's more. When Grace and I were having difficulty conceiving..." He drew in a long breath through a tight jaw. His back was ramrod straight. This was the moment of truth—he was breaking a vow he'd made to his dead wife. Matthew wasn't the kind of man who made vows easily, she knew. And he'd break them even less easily. Uncaring of the consequences this time, she moved to his side, freely giving whatever she could. His hand snaked out and wrapped around hers, squeezing her fingers tight. When he continued, his voice was even and strong. No one—who wasn't having their fingers squeezed to within an inch of their health— would guess this was hard for him.

"We found that Grace's eggs weren't able to be used. She went to Susannah again for help, and Susannah's eggs were used instead. Susannah is Flynn's biological mother."

There was silence in the room. Not a comment or clink of glass, or movement. Matthew's grasp on her fingers didn't ease. Despite wondering how his family was reacting to the news, to her, she kept her gaze on Matthew. He needed her.

"The reason Susannah has been here recently is when Flynn was in danger of needing a bone-marrow transplant, I wasn't an ideal donor because of my penicillin allergy. I called Susannah, and she graciously said she'd come to Charleston and do whatever we needed. She's been here on standby. In case Flynn needed her bone marrow."

Elizabeth was the first to move. She sprang out of her seat

and claimed Susannah in a fierce hug. "You did that for my grandson?"

"Well," Susannah stammered, surprised, "I didn't need to do anything in the end."

"But you came. And you were willing." Elizabeth stepped away, tears shining in her eyes. "Thank you."

RJ was next to grab her in a bear hug. "We all love that kid. Thanks for being here for him."

She was hugged and thanked by each Kincaid in turn, becoming a little disoriented and wobbly, but then, still in a hug from one of his sisters, a familiar hand clasped hers and she was grounded again, anchored in uneven waters. She glanced around the group, and something struck her. This family was unlike any of the society families she'd met with her grandparents. And they were nothing like her grandparents themselves. She'd been so wary of the Kincaids, so caught up in her expectations of wealthy, powerful families, that she'd allowed herself to be prejudiced. That was unfair. They were a warm, loving family.

"But why was this such a secret?" Elizabeth said when they'd settled again. "Why hide who Susannah is?"

Susannah turned to Elizabeth before Matthew could speak. This was one time she could save him the anguish of answering. "He was honoring Grace's wishes, and that took a lot of courage."

Matthew looked at her, and there was such emotion in his eyes that her heart missed a beat.

"You know," Elizabeth said, "I think lunch might be ready. Let's go into the dining room." More was said, but Susannah couldn't hear anything besides a background buzz. She was watching Matthew. He didn't move until the room was quiet, then he took her hand. "Will you come with me out into the garden?"

She knew he was going to ask her to stay here in Charleston. The way he'd almost asked earlier. Yet nothing had changed between them. She still loved him. He still wanted her, she had no doubt, but not the way she needed him to want her. If she had to refuse him again, she might just fall apart.

She was about to deflect the question, when he added, "I promise I won't ask you to stay again."

What else did they have to say to each other? Yet it was such a simple request and he was standing before her so tall and solid and *Matthew* that she couldn't find it inside herself to say no. A few more stolen moments together before her evening flight could hardly make things worse than they were.

With emotion clogging her throat, she nodded, and followed him out. They were deep in the elaborate gardens, a long way from the house when he stopped walking and turned to her.

"I need to say something to you, and you won't want to believe it, but please just listen anyway."

"Okay," she said warily.

There was silence for a long moment and she watched a line form between his brows, the dip of his Adam's apple. "You think I only see you as a replacement for Grace and you were probably right at the start."

"I didn't help, by trying to fit into your lives seamlessly."

"That was a blessing. At that time, with Flynn so unwell, I appreciated that more than I can say."

"But it meant you never saw me."

"I saw you," he said huskily. "I see you now."

"Matthew—"

"You're the woman who intuitively found my favorite place in the house to be alone."

She frowned, then understanding dawned as clear as the blue sky above them. "The wine cellar."

"The cellar has been the only place I can be me in that house. Sometimes I've needed that for five minutes. Not a father or a husband or, more recently, a widower. Just me. And you went there for the same reason, didn't you?"

"Yes," she whispered.

"And I didn't mind being there with you. Sharing it with you."

She went to speak again, but he placed a finger over her lips. "You're the woman who throws her arms out to the sky just to feel the breeze against her face. Who introduced me to pink grapefruit gelato and who cooks decadent desserts. Who has a strange fascination with my wrists and hands."

A smile wobbled on her lips. "I thought I was being subtle."

"You were. But I was watching you closely." He tenderly smoothed the hair back from her face. "I couldn't take my eyes off you. I still can't."

This was breaking her heart. She blinked, not knowing which way to turn, what to do or say. "Why are you making this more difficult?"

"You're the woman who stood up to her grandparents and forced them to treat her properly," he said as if she hadn't spoken. "Maybe the only person who's done that to the Larrimores, and they've come back to you and I'll bet money they'll be in your life again, but on your terms."

That was one charge she couldn't accept. She shook her head. "I'm not sure—"

He put the finger back over her lips. "You were magnificent in your strength with them."

A painful pressure was building behind her breastbone and she pushed a hand to it to ease the ache. It made no difference. "Please, Matthew." Her eyes burned with unshed tears.

"I see you, Susannah," he said with fierce certainty. "Maybe at the start I was foolish enough to let you slip into Grace's role in our family, but you're no replacement. You're Susannah, and I see you."

A tear slipped down her cheek. "Matthew…"

"Most important of all you're the woman I love."

Her heart turned over in her chest as she hardly dared to believe. "You said—"

"I swore I'd never love again," he said, cutting her off then he winced. "A stupid, stupid thing to say, to even think. I was trying to save myself from the hurt of the breakdown in my relationship with Grace, but being without you for these past few days...that's been worse than any pain I was trying to avoid."

"For me, too," she said, her lips quivering, happiness swelling within.

"Tell me one thing. Do you love me? Because if you don't, I swear I'll—"

With a tentative hand, she reached out and stroked the side of his face. "I love you, Matthew, almost more than my heart can bear."

"Susannah," he said in a thick voice, and crushed her in his arms. "I said I wouldn't ask you to stay, and I was serious." He stepped back, just holding her hands between his. "I want much more than you to merely stay. Marry me."

A shiver of delight ran down her spine then worked its way outward, till she was trembling all over. He saw the real her. He was willing to accept his love for her. It was too much...

"Marry me, Susannah Parrish, and make a life with me and Flynn." His brilliant green eyes were full of love and yearning. "And when I say make a life with us, I mean just that. Not the life we have now, but one we create together, that reflects all three of us. We can live anywhere, do anything. As long as we do it together."

"Yes," she said, but it only came out as a faint rasp. So she drew in a long breath and said it again, making sure it was as strong and sure as she felt. "Yes, Matthew Kincaid, I'll marry you. There's nothing in this world that could make me happier than to create a life with you and Flynn."

He picked her up and turned them in a circle before releasing her and kissing her. Everything inside her danced—the air was warmer on her skin, the sun shone more brightly. Matthew, *her Matthew,* loved her. Wanted to build a life with her.

Then she drew away. "And I promise you, I won't let Flynn

forget Grace. She loved him, and he needs to know that. But I have a question for you."

"Ask me anything," he said, emotion shining in his eyes.

"Since you've been watching me this closely and seem to know so much about me, did you know I'm pregnant with your child?"

His eyes widened and his jaw slackened. Then a grin split his face and he picked her up again. Laughter bubbled up her throat and out.

"I'd planned to tell you today, but I knew it was going to be hard for you to explain to your family about Flynn, so I wanted to let you do that first. I—"

"I don't care when you were going to tell me, as long as you did." He kissed her. "Flynn will be beside himself to have a little brother or sister."

She bit down on her smile, trying to be serious for a moment. "Matthew, I'm not very far along, so do you mind if we don't tell anyone yet?"

"Frankly that's one secret I'd be glad to keep for now."

And then he leaned down and kissed her with all the passion and honesty she'd ever hoped for.

* * * * *

Turn the page for an exclusive short story
by USA TODAY bestselling author Day Leclaire.

Then look for the next installment of
DYNASTIES: THE KINCAIDS,
BEHIND BOARDROOM DOORS,
by USA TODAY bestselling author Jennifer Lewis
wherever Harlequin books are sold.

THE KINCAIDS: JACK AND NIKKI, PART II
Day Leclaire

This was a mistake. This was a mistake. This was a *huge* mistake.

Nikki Thomas pushed the door to her office shut, tempted to lock it, as well. Unfortunately if someone dropped by, she'd be forced to explain, something she was unwilling to do. If only she hadn't made that outrageous bid at the bachelor charity auction for Read and Write, a local nonprofit organization that supported literacy in everyone from five to ninety-five. If only the man she'd bid on had been anyone other than Jack Sinclair.

But she had bid on Jack Sinclair, the most despised man in all Charleston, South Carolina. Jack Sinclair, the Kincaid bastard. Jack Sinclair, the direct competitor of The Kincaid Group, the firm she worked for as a corporate investigator. Jack Sinclair, the man who'd taken her in his arms one short month ago and kissed her senseless. Kissed her in a way she'd never, ever been kissed before. Kissed her in a way she wanted to be kissed again.

Soon.

Working up her courage, she crossed to her desk and placed

the call on her cell phone, preferring not to use the company landline to contact "the enemy." A moment later, a woman answered, clearly an admin. "Please connect me to Jack Sinclair," Nikki requested briskly.

"Certainly. May I ask who's calling and what it's regarding?"

"Nikki Thomas." That was the easy part. Answering the other question was the not-so-easy part and a ball of tension formed in the pit of her stomach. How could she be so cool and collected when it came to her job, and such a mess when it came to personal relationships? It didn't make any sense. "It's regarding… It's regarding an appointment Jack and I were forced to postpone." Okay, that would work. Enough information to get past the dragon at the gate, but not so much it caused undue comment.

"I'd be happy to help you with that appointment. I have Mr. Sinclair's calendar right here."

Damn. Not enough info to get past the dragon. "Thank you, but he asked that I speak to him directly. If you could just let him know I'm on the line?"

"Of course, Ms. Thomas."

Several minutes of silence ensued, long enough that the urge to simply hang up almost had her pressing the disconnect button at least half a dozen times. Before she could give in to impulse, Jack's dark, distinctive voice sounded in her ear. "Nikki?"

She closed her eyes, fighting back a shiver. If a voice could be a food, his would be dark, creamy Belgian chocolate, the sort that melted on the tongue and gave that delicious sensation of bittersweet richness. She fought to keep her voice calm and level, to hide the almost overwhelming need for a hit of the chocolate she was imagining.

"Hi, Jack." For some reason her voice came out low. Sultry.

"I thought you'd changed your mind about our date." His voice also sounded low. Sexy.

She managed a quick laugh. "Hey, I won you fair and square.

I'm not about to change my mind." Especially not after that mind-blowing kiss they'd shared.

"Paid top dollar for me, as I recall."

"A thousand of those top dollars, as *I* recall."

"I'll try to make it worth every penny. I gather you're ready to collect what you've won?"

His tone sounded lightly flirtatious suggesting she'd caught him alone in his office with a few minutes on his hands. A soft squeak came through the line, the sort of sound a desk chair made when tipped back. An image of him sprang to life. Corporate Jack, feet resting on the edge of his desk, wearing an expensive, tailored suit in a dense brown color that matched his hair, with a narrow pinstripe in a robin's egg blue to match his eyes. The shirt…? A crisp taupe with an expensive tie that picked up on the blue again. From what little she knew of him, he'd have loosened the knot of his tie, giving him an edge that blended business with a worldly casualness. A lion in his prime, secure in his position and able to overcome any threat. Heaven help her!

She hastened to answer his question. "I am ready to collect my winnings. I believe that's a night of dinner and dancing." She moistened her lips, going for broke. "Not to mention, a wish of my choice."

His soft chuckle had her practically melting in her chair. "Foolish on my part to throw that into the bargain. Do you want your wish, too, or just a date?"

Tempting. Oh, so tempting. "I think we'll stick with dinner and dancing for the time being."

"Is this weekend convenient?"

She made a pretense of flipping through her calendar book, though she doubted it fooled him. "Actually that would be perfect."

"Shall we say Saturday? I'll pick you up at six."

"Great." A knock sounded on her door, distracting her. "I'll see you then, Jack."

His laugh rang in her ear, stirring the most outrageous sensations. "You've forgotten one small detail."

Matthew Kincaid, Director of New Business for The Kincaid Group, stood in the doorway, and she waved him in, dismayed by his presence. Not someone she wanted to overhear this particular conversation. "What detail have I forgotten?" she asked Jack.

"Where do I pick you up?"

"Oh, right." She rattled off the address. "I'll see you then."

"Someone just walked into your office, didn't they?"

"Is it that obvious?" she asked, wry humor sliding through the question.

"I can hear it in your voice. As tempted as I am to tease you about it, I'll play the part of the gentleman and let you go. See you Saturday."

"I look forward to it." She disconnected the call and turned her attention to Matthew and smiled. "Hey, stranger. Good to see you back at work. How's Flynn doing?"

His expression relaxed into a grin. He'd suffered one of the most terrifying ordeals any parent could face when his three-year-old son had developed aplastic anemia following a strong viral infection. Fortunately, the medication Flynn received to treat the disease worked. If it hadn't, his biological mother, Susannah, was waiting in the wings to donate her bone marrow. Her timely appearance had also led to a romance between her and Matthew, one soon heading to the altar. "Better and better, thanks."

"I hear congratulations are in order." She smiled with sincere pleasure. "I couldn't be happier for you and Susannah."

"I'm still in shock. A happy sort of shock, since it's still sinking in."

"I hope you'll bring her by and introduce us. From everything I've heard, your fiancée is a special woman."

"She is that."

"So, what's up? Did you have something you needed me to do for you?"

"A potential client I'd like you to check out." He handed her a file. "I definitely don't want to turn away business if I can help it. But I also want to be smart about it."

"Understandable." She flipped open the file and scanned the details. "I'll get right on this. When do you need to get back to them?"

"Monday."

"No problem. I'll have it to you by Friday."

He hesitated, warning that she probably wouldn't like the next topic of conversation. Sure enough, he asked, "I don't suppose that was Jack Sinclair you were talking to? I heard you mention his name when I first knocked."

Nikki lifted a shoulder in a casual shrug. "I won dinner with him at the Read and Write literacy auction. We've had a little trouble coordinating our schedules."

"So, you're not dating him?"

A tiny flare of temper curled through her at the intrusion into her private affairs, but she kept her voice calm and even. "This will be our first." She tilted her head to one side. "Is that a problem?"

"Could be." He lowered his voice. "You know who he is, Nikki. The damage he's already caused the family. The damage he could cause The Kincaid Group. You work here, which makes you as vulnerable as the rest of us if he takes over and decides to clean house."

"I doubt that will happen. RJ's in line to—"

"You're right. RJ *is* in line to step into Dad's shoes. But considering Sinclair owns forty-five percent of TKG stock, there's no guarantee it'll happen. I guess the board will decide that during the annual meeting in June." His green eyes narrowed. "But now that I think about it, you might be in a position to help."

She stiffened. Did he know her secret? Is that why he was

asking for her help? No, no. It wasn't possible. No one knew.
She forced herself to relax. "What can I do?" she asked simply.

"You're going out with him on this date, right?" He kept his
gaze trained on her, his expression reflecting his determination.
"Maybe he'll say something to you, give you some idea about
his intentions."

"That doesn't make sense, Matthew. Why would he confide
in me?"

"He doesn't know you work for us, right? Maybe you could
bring up the subject, see if Sinclair says anything that might
help us figure out his plans."

She shook her head even before he finished speaking. "Please
don't ask me to spy for you. I don't do business that way."

"Think about it, Nikki. Think long and hard." He planted his
hands on her desk and leaned in, not in a threatening way, more
as a way to underscore his conviction. "While you're enjoying
dinner with Sinclair, listen to him. Get a feel for the man. Is
he someone you want in charge of TKG? He's our competitor.
There's no way he won't attempt to fold TKG into Carolina Shipping. If I'm wrong and you think he's on the up-and-up, fine.
But if you get the impression he's as ruthless as we've heard…"

She hesitated, then nodded. "I'll think about it, Matthew. No
promises."

"Fair enough."

But the idea of spying on Jack Sinclair made her squirm despite feeling a strong allegiance to the Kincaids, particularly to
Reginald Kincaid, who'd literally saved her professional repu-
tation when her ex-fiancé had ripped it to shreds. Still… Would
it be so awful to just listen to Jack and ask a few questions to
draw him out? And if Jack happened to say something helpful,
was there really any harm in passing it along? She blew out a
sigh, knowing full well what she'd do, that she'd use whatever
investigative skills available to help the Kincaids.

Nikki closed her eyes, letting go of what might have been.
Letting go of possibilities. It was a darn shame. In the short

time she'd spent with Jack, they'd hit it off. Not to mention the key element that had kept her fantasizing about him for a solid month.

Jack really was a fantastic kisser.

Jack arrived at Nikki's door promptly at six. To his surprise, he realized he was looking forward to seeing her again, to discovering if the attraction he'd felt the night of the bachelor auction remained, or if it had faded in the month since they'd been apart. One thing that continued to linger in his memory was that kiss they'd shared.

He couldn't remember the last time he'd felt such an explosive reaction to a woman, nor experienced such a deep, unremitting want. Even after so long he continued to puzzle over it, unable to explain what made her so different from other women he'd known. He was simply forced to accept one indisputable fact. He wanted her, wanted her more than anyone else he'd ever kissed. She represented a tantalizing interlude to call to mind whenever the stress of business—or the Kincaids—grew too severe, which was just about every damn day.

He released a short, mocking laugh, calling himself every kind of fool. He'd built a brief encounter up in his mind, fantasizing it into something it wasn't, and never could be. Ridiculous, really.

Tonight, he'd escort the very attractive Nikki Thomas to his home for a candlelit evening of dinner and dancing. They might exchange another kiss or two. He doubted it would go anywhere from there. Then he'd return her safely to her doorstep. And that would be the end of that. Maybe at some point down the road she'd call about this ridiculous wish he'd promised to grant. Chances were, she wouldn't bother. It had been more in the way of a joke. After that, he'd get down to the serious business of destroying the Kincaids, before they could destroy him. Story over.

He found a parking space close to her Rainbow Row house,

a miracle in itself, and exited his Aston Martin Volante. He approached the front door and knocked, surprised when it swung open almost immediately. It was then that Jack realized three very important facts.

One. His fantasies had been all wrong. Nikki Thomas was far more beautiful than he remembered.

Two. If the evening ended any other way than with her in his bed, he might just go insane.

And three. One night with her couldn't possibly come close to satisfying him.

She stood before him in a flirty little dress, the brilliant sapphire-blue perfectly matching the color of her eyes. She wore her hair up in a loose knot, a few wayward tendrils escaping to caress the creamy skin of her neck—creamy skin he wanted to taste. Badly.

"Right on time. I like that about a man," she said with a warm smile.

"Almost as much as I appreciate promptness in a woman."

"Sounds like we're in agreement." Her smile grew, drawing his attention to the lush mouth he planned to consume at his earliest possible opportunity. "At least on this point."

"An excellent start."

Taking his hand in hers, she leaned in and kissed the corner of his mouth. Instantly the want he'd been holding in check slammed through him. Without a word, he yanked her close, took her mouth with a passion that caused wildfire to burst into flames between them. He didn't even remember slamming the door closed or maneuvering her backward, just felt the dull thud when they hit the wall and her soft gasp that allowed him to slip inside her warm, sweet mouth.

He half expected her to protest the taking. Instead her arms wound around his neck and she tugged him closer, her soft moan threatening to unman him. His hands swept over her, tracing the impressive curves her dress displayed. Naked. He wanted her naked and under him. To hell with dinner. Instead they'd consume each other. Make love here and now.

Before he could act, she spun away, drawing in a deep, shaky breath. "Okay, that answers that question." She snatched up a knee-length black wool coat that hid every scrap of her from view. "Shall we go?" she asked, though he caught a ripple of turbulence racing through her words.

"No. Stay." It was all he could manage.

She took a swift step away from him, a deep feminine vulnerability darkening her eyes. "I don't think that's smart."

Before he could stop her, she opened the door and stepped out into the brisk February breeze, leaving him no choice but to follow. He waited while she locked her front door and fought to regain his self-control, shocked by the lack of it. The cold helped clear his head and when she turned, he was able to gesture toward the Aston Martin with something approaching normalcy. She paused on the sidewalk to admire the sleek lines of the ruby-red car.

"Impressive." She spared him a swift look, one that held the shocked echo of the kiss they'd just shared. Well, at least he wasn't the only one. Thank God for that much. "All of Charleston will know it's you whether you're coming or going."

He inclined his head. "That's the idea." He opened the passenger door, admiring the graceful way Nikki slid in. Admiring even more the flash of long, toned legs, accentuated by a pair of mile-high heels. He was fast creating a Nikki "to do" list and seeing her naked in those heels just topped it. "You haven't asked where we're going," he commented as soon as he'd climbed behind the steering wheel.

"I like surprises. Most of the time, at least."

"Let's hope that kiss was one of the surprises you liked. Most of the time."

She hesitated for an unnerving moment, then admitted, "I think you can safely put a check in the 'like' box." She moistened her lips in a way that suggested she could still taste him. "Will I like this next surprise?"

"I hope so, though there's no way it can compare to kissing you." The engine started with a low, muted roar. "This surprise has to do with tonight's venue. To be honest, I considered taking you home."

"And where is home?"

"Greenville."

Her brows shot up. "That's a mile or so down the road."

"About two hundred of them," he confirmed. "But then I decided we'd spend the entire date driving and as much as I'd enjoy talking to you, I'd prefer putting those hours to a much better use."

Her magnificent eyes narrowed. "And to what use do you plan to put them?"

He slowed for a red light and pulled to a stop before responding. "With you in my arms." He flicked her a quick glance before the light changed. She didn't bother to conceal a certain level of wariness and he forced himself to throttle back when every part of him demanded he punch the gas. "Dancing, of course. Naturally that meant a change of venue was in order."

"Naturally."

"But I still wanted to take you home. So…"

"So?" she prompted.

"We'll settle for my home away from home. Since my company is based in Charleston, it's impractical to commute to and from Greenville every day."

"Makes sense." She leaned back against her seat, continuing to regard him through narrowed eyes.

"What?" he asked.

"Just trying to decide what sort of place you'd own."

"Here…or in Greenville?"

She waved a hand through the air. "Oh, the Greenville one is easy."

Bull. "And what sort of place do you think I'd own in Greenville?"

"A magnificent plantation," she answered promptly. "Gracious Southern living at its best. A blend of past and present, beautifully restored. And I imagine the interior is a blend, as well, antiques mated with classic contemporary. Am I close?"

"Damn." She was better than he'd anticipated.

She chuckled. "I'm good at reading people."

"I'll consider myself forewarned."

"But I forgot the most important part."

"Which is?"

"You'd want to put your own mark on the place in some way. Probably a way that had your interior decorator most unhappy."

"Now I'm seriously impressed." And he was. "What about my Charleston place?"

"Mmm. More difficult," she admitted. "I'm guessing it would need to be large enough to entertain. Considering the car you drive, you like a bit of flash. Yet, elegant flash. You wouldn't settle for anything that didn't have a view of the water. I'm thinking you went in the opposite direction with your Charleston home. Modern. Contemporary. All the comforts, but less Old World. Am I close?"

"No."

"Well, shoot." Her luscious mouth turned downward, tempting him beyond reason to kiss her again. "Where did I go wrong?"

"You didn't. You weren't close, you're dead-on. Again." He spared her a swift glance. "You researched me, didn't you?"

Her blatant surprise answered for her, even before she shook her head in automatic denial. "I really didn't. It's a game I used to play with my father. He's a cop. Was a cop," she corrected.

"That's right. You mentioned he's in law enforcement." Then her correction sank in. "*Was* in law enforcement?"

"Died in the line of duty," she explained with painful brevity.

"I'm sorry."

"So was my family." She made an effort to throw off the shadows. "When I was little we'd play this game where we'd see strangers at a restaurant or in the park and we'd try to figure out things about them based on what we observed. Sometimes my father would go over and identify himself in order to see how close we'd come."

"People didn't mind?"

"You know, they never did. Dad just had this way about him. He could put people at their ease." She tossed him a broad grin. "Or scare them spitless. You didn't dare lie to my father. He could smell it a mile away. He'd just stare at you with those cop's eyes of his and the truth would come tumbling out, willy-nilly."

"Sounds like a man I'd have enjoyed getting to know."

She tilted her head in his direction. "No secrets to hide? He was hell on secrets, I can tell you."

"None worth mentioning," he replied smoothly.

"Huh. I think you're a first."

"In what way?"

"I don't think I've ever met a man without secrets."

They'd arrived at his oceanfront home, saving him from commenting further. It was exactly as she'd described. Instead of pulling into the garage, he parked by the walkway leading to the front steps. Ankle-high lights edged the curving ribbon of slate, tucked discreetly into the strip of garden that bracketed each side. Short, neatly trimmed bushes stood sentry duty along the edge of the garden and Nikki suspected that in the spring and summer a wealth of flowers added color and texture.

He opened the door for her and she stepped into a large, open foyer. On the far side, a great room cascaded toward the back of the house where a wall of windows overlooked the ocean. An enormous stone fireplace occupied one end of the space, complete with cheerfully crackling fire. Comfortable sofas and wing chairs grouped themselves in a loose semicircle around the hearth. Nearby, a table covered in snowy-white linen had been placed in front of the glass wall in preparation for their meal.

"Would you care for a drink?" he asked.

"Yes, please." She wandered deeper into the great room. "This is a gorgeous place, Jack. Perfect for entertaining."

"It's also perfect for intimate dinners for two." He handed her a glass of wine, the deep ruby color combining with the scent of berry, spice and herbs. "Thank you for bidding on me. I hope you'll find the evening well worth what you paid."

"I'm sure I will." She touched her glass to his, the crystal singing melodically. She took a sip of the creamy wine and smiled in appreciation. "I don't think I've tasted anything quite like it."

"It's a Spanish Termanthia I discovered a few years ago. A little exotic. But the spices in the Cantonese meal we're having tonight pair well with it."

"Sounds delicious."

As it was. The meal was catered, the waitstaff gliding in and out so efficiently, she barely noticed their presence. The conversation never lagged. The diciest moment came when he asked what she did for a living.

"I'm a corporate investigator," she answered, keeping her tone easy and off-the-cuff. "I specialize in background checks, illegal activities on the part of employees, corporate espionage. That sort of thing."

"Interesting." She'd captured his interest. "Do you also work the financial end of things?"

"Sometimes, though that's not my primary area of expertise. We have a CPA to handle that aspect, though I often work in conjunction with him. If he suspects fraudulent billing on the part of a supplier, I might go undercover and look into it. But for the most part my job involves a lot of computer time and pushing paper around." She helped herself to a final bite of stir-fry before deliberating nudging the plate aside. If she ate any more she risked exploding, but man, it had been good. "What about you? You own Carolina Shipping, right?"

"So, you did research me."

She picked up her wineglass and swirled the contents. "Which sounds worse, that I researched you…or that I listened to local gossip?" She drank, returned the glass to the table and relaxed back in her chair. "It's hard to go anywhere these days without hearing about you and the Kincaids."

"So, you know who I am."

"Yes. And I know about your connection to the Kincaid family."

His mouth tightened. "Congratulations. You win the award for finding the most polite way of calling me Reginald Kincaid's bastard I've ever heard. I'm surprised, knowing who I am, that you still came tonight."

She lifted an eyebrow, decided to be blunt. "Was I supposed to cancel because you're a bastard?"

"I wouldn't have been surprised."

She gave him a direct look. "The only way I would have canceled is if you'd been a bastard in actuality rather than in birth. Does that clarify the matter?"

"I believe it does."

He fell silent while their plates were whisked away. Then he stood and held out his hand. Unresisting, she took it, allowed him to tug her from her chair. She stepped into his arms without any hesitation and lifted her face to his. Where before their kiss had been frantic and beyond passionate, now it was slow and leisurely. The flames were there, no question about that, but carefully banked toward a long, slow burn.

She could taste the wine they'd consumed, taste the delicate blend of spices that had flavored their dinner and now flavored their kiss. This time when his hands skimmed over her curves, they were thorough rather than desperate, inching the gauge of her need to steadily higher and higher levels. Aware that they were fast approaching the point of no return, she pulled back and stared up at him.

He wasn't handsome in the conventional sense. His features were too hard for that, hacked into strong, ruthless lines by birth and circumstances that had toughened him through trial by fire. And yet, he appealed on some elemental level, male to female. He called to her, filled her with a longing she'd never experienced before, left her trembling with a feminine vulnerability that terrified her. He must have read some of her reaction because he cupped her face with a gentleness she'd never have guessed him capable of.

"I requested that they put dessert in the refrigerator for later," he informed her. "If you'd prefer it now...?"

"Not a chance. I'm stuffed." Then she keyed in on what he'd said and eyed him uncertainly. "Later?"

A small flame kindled in his gaze. "How does key-lime tart sound...for breakfast?"

She exhaled a long sigh of hesitation. "Complicated."

"Is that a yes, or a no?"

She closed her eyes and faced the truth. Whatever was going on between them was long past complicated. Not that it changed anything. She looked at him. Wanted him. And felt her helpless surrender. "That's a yes. In fact, it's a hell, yes."

* * * * *

PASSION

Harlequin

Desire

COMING NEXT MONTH
AVAILABLE MARCH 13, 2012

#2143 TEMPTED BY HER INNOCENT KISS
Pregnancy & Passion
Maya Banks

#2144 BEHIND BOARDROOM DOORS
Dynasties: The Kincaids
Jennifer Lewis

#2145 THE PATERNITY PROPOSITION
Billionaires and Babies
Merline Lovelace

#2146 A TOUCH OF PERSUASION
The Men of Wolff Mountain
Janice Maynard

**#2147 A FORBIDDEN
AFFAIR**
The Master Vintners
Yvonne Lindsay

**#2148 CAUGHT IN
THE SPOTLIGHT**
Jules Bennett

You can find more information on upcoming
Harlequin® titles, free excerpts and more at
www.Harlequin.com.

HDCNM0212

There came a time in a man's life when he knew he was well and truly caught. Devon Carter stared down at the diamond ring nestled in velvet and acknowledged that this was one such time. He snapped the lid closed and shoved the box into the breast pocket of his suit.

He had two choices. He could marry Ashley Copeland and fulfill his goal of merging his company with Copeland Hotels, thus creating the largest, most exclusive line of resorts in the world, or he could refuse and lose it all.

Put in that light, there wasn't much he could do except pop the question.

The doorman to his Manhattan high-rise apartment hurried to open the door as Devon strode toward the street. He took a deep breath before ducking into his car, and the driver pulled into traffic.

Tonight was the night. All of his careful wooing, the countless dinners, kisses that started brief and casual and became more breathless—all a lead-up to tonight. Tonight his seduction of Ashley Copeland would be complete, and then he'd ask her to marry him.

He shook his head as the absurdity of the situation hit him for the hundredth time. Personally, he thought William Copeland was crazy for forcing his daughter down Devon's throat.

Ashley was a sweet enough girl, but Devon had no desire

to marry anyone.

William had other plans. He'd told Devon that Ashley had no head for the family business. She was too softhearted, too naive. So he'd made Ashley part of the deal. The catch? Ashley wasn't to know of it. Which meant Devon was stuck playing stupid games.

Ashley was supposed to think this was a grand love match. She was a starry-eyed woman who preferred her animal-rescue foundation over board meetings, charts and financials for Copeland Hotels.

If she ever found out the truth, she wouldn't take it well.

And hell, he couldn't blame her.

But no matter the reason for his proposal, before the night was over, she'd have no doubts that she belonged to him.

What will happen when Devon marries Ashley?
Find out in Maya Banks's passionate new novel
TEMPTED BY HER INNOCENT KISS
Available March 2012 from Harlequin Desire!

USA TODAY bestselling author

Carol Marinelli

begins a daring duet.

THE SECRETS
of
XANOS

Two brothers alike in charisma and power;
separated at birth and seeking revenge...

Nico has always felt like an outsider. He's turned his back on his
parents' fortune to become one of Xanos's most powerful exports
and nothing will stand in his way—until he stumbles
upon a virgin bride....

Zander took his chances on the streets rather than spending another
moment under his cruel father's roof. Now he is unrivaled in
business—and the bedroom! He wants the best people around him,
and Charlotte is the best PA! Can he tempt her
over to the dark side...?

A SHAMEFUL CONSEQUENCE
Available in March

AN INDECENT PROPOSITION
Available in April

www.Harlequin.com

HP13053